FREUD AND HIS LONG JOURNEY

INTO DEATH

Lúcio Roberto Marzagão
Translator: A.H. Lin

FREUD AND HIS LONG JOURNEY INTO DEATH

1ª Edição
POD

Petrópolis
KBR
2013

Text Editing **Noga Sklar**
1st Edition copyediting **Rachel Kopit Cunha**
Translation **A.H. Lin**
Cover design **KBR over Salvador Dali's drawing**
Images **Google Archive**

ISBN: 978-85-8180-137-7

KBR Editora Digital Ltda.
www.kbrdigital.com.br
atendimento@kbrdigital.com.br
55|24|2222.3491

150 - Psychology

 **Lúcio Roberto Marzagão** has a Master's Degree in Philosophy from UFMG (Minas Gerais, Brazil), where he has been an Associate Professor for 30 years. Presently he is a teacher at the *Lato Sensu* Postgraduate Program in Psychoanalytic Theory at UFMG. He also published *Psicanálise e Pragmática*, in 1966, and with KBR the 2nd edition of *Psicanálise e Literatura*, in 2012.

Email: luciomarzagao@gmail.com

Be absolute for death; either death or life
Shall thereby be the sweeter. Reason thus with life:
If I do lose thee, I do lose a thing
That none but fools would keep: a breath thou art,
Servile to al the skyey influences,
That dost this habitation, where thou keep'st
Hourly afflict: merely, thou art death's fool;
For him thou larour'st by thy flight to shun
And yet runn'st toward him still.

William Shakespeare, "Measure for Measure",
Act 3, scene 1

For Lúcia, Cristiana, and Raquel

I should expressly mention the collaboration I received from the Specialization Course in Psychoanalytic Theory at UFMG in the person of its coordinator, Professor Eduardo Dias Gontijo, and from the Sigmund Freud Museum of London in the person of its curator, Michael Molnar.

I would like to mention all the people directly or indirectly involved in this project. I have concluded that my gratitude is vaster than the limits of this text. My friends and colleagues, each in his own way, gave an immeasurable contribution.

Sumário

PREFACE

Freud is dying. Memories, ideas, scenes from his long life are passing through his mind. The physical pain is unbearable. As agreed to years before, Dr. Max Schur has administered a lethal injection of morphine. Freud's last thought at the sight of Death approaching: *Heads I win; tails, you lose...*

Once he wrote to Wilhelm Fliess that deep down he wished he were neither a physician nor a scientist: "*Ich bin ein conquistador,*" like Pizarro or Cortes. Lucio Marzagão's very original re-creation of the great man's final months captures this essential facet of Freud's character. If it were approached in an academic manner, the volume would list references; it would parade all Freud's biographies, testimonials by people who knew him, and collections of letters written by him and to him—all scholarship of the best quality. However, this author employs his erudition with a non-academic grace and levity, honoring the tradition of excellent writing by the sons and daughters of the State of Minas Gerais.

To tell his story, the author employs a great variety of resources: He alternates internal monologue with letters to Martha or Princess Marie Bonaparte; there are "reminiscences" of the family's employee, Paula Fichtl, "interviews" given to an English journalist, dialogues with Dr. Schur and with

Anna Freud—affectionately called Annerl—and so forth. Lucidity and humor, which Freud had in abundance, glitter on each page, though mixed with a certain pessimism and resignation.

When he told the Princess that his legacy would last for at most thirty years, Freud was completely wrong. Without a doubt, in the coming decades psychoanalysis will continue to interest many people as it does today, and texts like this the reader holds in his hand prove that imagination, tempered with scrupulous attention to the psychological events, can bear unexpected fruits.

"Fine cookie," Brazilian writer Oswald de Andrade would say, to be enjoyed like milk sweets and cheese-bread.

Renato Mezan
Psychoanalyst, São Paulo

THE END

Tuesday, September 19, 1939

I awake and immediately remembered what I wrote in what would be, I would suppose, my last letter to Princess Marie: "A small island of pain floating on an ocean of indifference." Some months later, I cannot make the same statement. The small island has become a continent. It has spread out in concentric circles and invaded every corner of my body. My body is a continent surrounded by people's attention. Their compassionate expressions display well-meaning concern. I live at the painful division between my decrepit body, progressively less responsive, failing body and my mind, still attentive and thoughtful. Feeling like a stranger in my own body, I am at the end; but I know that in these last moments I will not shrink in fear from death. During my life, I sought consistency, at the same time delighting in inevitable change. When I talked with Lou and Rilke, I sometimes argued that the true beauty of life resides in the constant change of the tree's clothing with each season. Through the window I can see that the Gregorian calendar prevails outside: Autumn is beginning. But inside this room I have no doubt that my winter approaches.

The pain is indescribable. It comes as a great irony: All my life I professed that the true liberation of the soul comes from transforming pains, feelings, and affects into words; but now that it is my turn, I can't manage to focus my attention. The pain has claimed everything for itself, everything.

Without exception, everyone in the house was exhausted. I had to submit to many different, humiliating medical procedures. But, as if there were a tacit agreement among us all, one moment we would deny the gravity of the illness and laugh together; at the next moment, our smiles came framed by dejection. I saved my tearful wails of sadness for sleepless early mornings. During my life, I have cried very few times; but when Sophie and my grand-son left, the pain of loss was truly beyond my capacity to endure.

Freud and Sophie.

I hope that if I kept my eyes closed, the pain would diminish as it does when I hold still. It has become increasingly difficult to speak. Few of them can make sense of my sighs or the words I carefully form with swollen, sore lips. Paula manages to understand, especially when I ask for something simple. At times, Annerl makes out occasional comments. Martha watches closely with her arms crossed over her heart to contain her racing heartbeat, but she comprehends very little of what I say. Minna's illness prevents her from leaving her bedroom on the floor above, but she sends messages. Max—for many years my physician and now my confidante—has returned from the United States and moved to Maresfield Gardens. He now stands at my headboard, looking from side to side like a soldier guarding and important place against an imaginary enemy.

"Guten Morgen, Herr Professor, Entschuldigung." With

these cheerful words, my beloved Paula enters the room. Her discerning eyes scan my bed and debilitated body. She approaches. Almost whispering, I tell her that we no longer have to speak in German. A year has passed since we received an unforgettable reception bordering on veneration. As for the deference to me as a professor, I insist she never again address me in this way. Austria and its rulers would not permit it. And breakfast can wait. I no longer care about time. I learned to pay attention to details, and I know that some details, like eating, for example, are now irrelevant.

Time always ordered my activities. Now, I busy myself with self-observation. I respond, "Hello, Miss Paula!" With both of her legs leaning against my bed, she draws near my head, adjusts my pillow, pulls up a chair, and sits close to me face. Holding a bowl with hot steaming broth, she delicately lifts my head and, without speaking, fills the spoon. I accept the soup, but can't recognize the taste of the broth. I wave the spoon to say thank you and pretend that I taste the broth. In truth, I like her taking care of me.

During the final days, I notice that my breathing had become progressively more labored. I no longer have control of my sphincters—a humiliating development that mimics my father's final suffering. Max has told me that my blood sugar is altered, so on top of everything else, I am absorbing food slowly. The broth feels hot in my mouth; and when I swallow, it energizes me. With effort, I turn to young Paula's compassionate face. I try to smile and want the smile to communicate my gratitude. Paula is part of my family. It took some time for the other women—Martha, Anna, and Minna—to accept her ways; but now she has earned everyone's admiration, even that of friends and colleagues living in Europe and the United States.

With open eyes, I watch Annerl enter. As always she

seems to be restless. She inspects the room as if she were a supervisor, looking for something out of place. When she looks me in the eye, I understand that she has been waiting for my pain to pass. She greets me affectionately, asks about my sleep; and, when I don't respond, she understands immediately. She looks at Paula inquisitively, and with her look, Paula answers that everything is good. Paula leaves the room, taking the bowl.

"Hello, daughter. Did you sleep well?

"Yes, father, but I can't get accustomed to the noise from Finchley Road. The busses never sleep. Was the broth good? I am sure you would prefer some eggs, tartar sauce, ham, and vanilla ice cream, but you can't eat ice cream in the morning, and liquid foods will be more easily absorbed. When you are better, we will have ham and toast."

We look at each other and understand that this day will never come.

I look at Anna and in a weak voice tell her that I would like to ask a favor.

"Sure, Papa. What is it?"

"I should respond to a friend's letter. I want to dictate it. Would that be possible?"

"A letter? Now is not the best time. . ."

"Well, Annerl, when it comes to a friend, I always respond to letters. It is for Albrecht Schaeffer, a German writer who wrote to me about mythology and mysticism, and translated Oscar Wilde, Diderot, and Verlaine into German. He is also moving to the United States."

"Very well, Papa, dictate it."

"Thank you."

"Dear Mr. Schaeffer,
What an unexpected and welcomed letter! I have

thought of my poet often in recent times, empty in some ways, asking myself how these wildly turbulent recent events in your birthplace have affected you! It brought me great pleasure to know that what I feared did not happen and that you found a precious partner in your wife.

"You would not be pleased to hear everything I could tell you about myself, but I am eighty-three years old. Therefore, the fact is my time has passed, and nothing remains for me to do except to follow the advice of your poem: Hope, Hope.

"Cordially yours,"

"Annerl, put this letter in the mail, today if possible."

The doorbell rings, and Anna immediately explains that it might be Professor Ernest Jones, who yesterday said that he would make a quick visit before seeing his patients. Instead, the barber enters the bedroom and begins to sharpen his razor, while talking about the war and England's hesitation to enter the conflict.

"Cowardice," he says.

Then he mechanically spreads the foam on my face, and I see that when he scrapes the right side of my face, he does it very slowly and cautiously, with special care to the surgical scars. I note, too, that he holds his breath while standing close to my face. As a matter of fact, everyone does that, including my dog, which is lying further and further from my bed... After a few minutes, the barber hurries out,

Freud and Ferenczi in 1917.

said good-bye and explaining that his schedule is full of appointments.

I am sitting in a chaise-long on the deck of a ship, smoking, and watching the limitless ocean... I am afraid and at the same time feel that I am ready to achieve glory and recognition... Jung and Ferenczi draw close... They say something I cannot understand... Jung moves in front of me and impedes my view of the water and the horizon... I move my head, and he moves again, still in front of me... I am irritated... I wake up.

Marie Bonaparte, Melanie Klein, Anna Freud, and Ernest Jones. Photo by Edward Bibring.

Once again, the doorbell interrupts my torpor. After a few minutes, Ernest and Anna enter the room. He wears a dark suit and tie, elegant as always, and greets me in a strong and optimistic voice. I greet Jones, slowly lifting my arms in

a sign of discouragement. He takes a seat in the same chair Paula had used a few minutes before and begins to talk about the British Psychoanalytic Society. I silently listen to his worry about the exile of the psychoanalysts from the continent, whether forced or voluntary. Many are Jews, and the British psychoanalysts are feeling threatened. Without speaking, I wonder if Jones might be anti-Semitic. *I cannot interpret his statement in this way. My reception by the English suggests the opposite,* I thought. Knowing that Ernest does not want to hear my opinion, I make an ambiguous gesture, agreeing with his words, and I allow drowsiness to overtake me once more. That would be Jones' last visit. I have become profoundly averse to political problems of any sort. I am only concerned with my daughter's professional future and with a solution to her problems with Mrs. Klein. I never know if my daily sleep reduces my fatigue or makes it worse.

After some time, I open my eyes. The bedroom is empty. My gaze passes over the bookcase, a small four-step ladder that has served me throughout my entire life, the divan, and easy chair, all the instruments of work; there among them, I recall laments, cries, and laughter. The hearth is dark, and I think that I will never again see it lit and crackling. Some of the books, my daily companions, are worn from constant use. Others wait their turn. The antiques... a lot of pain... everything has a story, evidence of my interest in archeology and other sciences, and most were given me by friends and colleagues. The value of the pieces is incalculable to me; as a collection, it is worth little. I look at each of them and visualize the person who gave it to me, the occasion, and what the piece means. In the cupboard which houses the collection, a Greco-roman vase stands out—a present from Princess Marie Bonaparte—a vase which was used to hold wine or honey and decorated by figures of people in ritual offe-

rings. It is my favorite piece. I am interested in the archeological value of the pieces, but at that moment, they reveal other meanings, principally the artistic. Finally, I look at the writing desk, where I have written about discoveries concerning the soul, discoveries which threatened people. At times, I paid dearly for that small piece of luck.

Everyone around me knows and remains cautiously silent about my approaching death, drawing closer with each moment. The movements around me grow increasingly theatrical. I act, and my small audience always responds as expected. I protect myself from this unpleasantness by sleeping or pretending to sleep, and everyone pretends to believe I am sleeping.

Now always silenced by the pain, I reflect over the past and the future of the science which I have conceived. Will posterity think of my work as literature or science? Will I be compared to Shakespeare or to Darwin?

I realize that it is September 19. On this day, especially in Italy, the Catholic church celebrates St. Gennaro, a martyr buried in Naples whose blood is preserved in small bottles and liquifies on this day every year. Despite my lack of faith, on certain occasions I used St. Gennaro and a poem by Virgil to argue with a skeptical colleague about the undeniable existence of the Unconscious. On such an occasion, I asked my friend to recite the poem, and he forgot the word, *aliquis.* I told him that his forgetting was not casual, but caused. Actually I am certain that psychoanalysis will not be accepted by force of argument, but rather by the patient's life experience. I consider the rest of the debate useless and tiring.

Nostalgic for the recent past, I reminisced about when

I walked slowly down the street at Maresfield Gardens to the avenue that had a metro station. Nearby, there was a cigar store where the proprietor knew of my routine and my addiction. When he saw me approaching, he waved, smiled, and spoke in slow, understandable English. He immediately offered me a box of cigars. I paid and thanked him, as if it were a present. On the way back, I watched the movement of cars and people; I responded mechanically to the greetings of those I knew and those I didn't. I arrived home, lit a cigar and from time to time gazed at it at arm's length and lost myself in the fragrant smoke. Since the age of twenty-four, cigars have always been my companions, as much as the books. Besides helping me work, they helped me concentrate. One time, I told my grandson, Harry, that I couldn't understand the fact that he didn't smoke since that was my greatest and cheapest entertainment. I smoked progressively less. I eventually smoked around twenty cigars per day. The scene during the Society meetings was comical. Everyone there held a cigar, all the time talking about psychoanalytic theory. People say that on one occasion, when faced with a colleague's insistence about the psychological meaning of a cigar, I told him that at times a cigar is only a cigar! When someone reminds me of this, I respond that I don't remember having written or said anything like that.

I puff and return to rereading *Moses and Monotheism*. I think about death: A human being spends a good part of his life trying to deny death, his own or the death of the people he loves. Without a doubt, writing books or creating works of art are among the activities that facilitate mourning our losses. With shocking ingenuousness, children ask their mothers, "When you die, should I do... [this or that]? Well, everyone knows the phrase, *"si vis pace, para bellum."* (*If you seek peace, prepare for war.*) I prefer, " *si vis vitam, para mortem"* (*If you want to live, prepare for death.*)

I see Max's face, distressed and hurried. Two weeks ago, more specifically, on September 3, a Sunday, England declared war on Germany. Max was in the garden where I was sunning myself and reading journals. He told me that the sirens were not a simple training exercise and moved me to the office on the ground floor as a precaution. So, there I was, looking at furniture, my collected objects. I remembered Shaw saying, "Don't try to live forever. It can't be done!"

When with eyes closed, I sense that no one is in the room, I surrender myself to daydreams and digressions. One more time, my increasingly cloudy consciousness returns to those holidays that I enjoyed on Austria's border with Italy, in the Dolomite Mountains in San Martino de Castrozza. As I said, I talked with my friends Lou Andréas-Salomé and Rilke. They complained about the transitory nature of life, and I argued that the beauty of life derived precisely from the changes, the cycles, and overcoming difficulties. And one more time, I am here, fighting against death, and for the second time on the same day, remembering the episode.

Rilke with Lou Andreas-Salomé in 1897, on the porch of the Andreas family summer home.

The sound made by a troop of soldiers marching down the road makes me think about war. I continued fighting in Vienna for dozens of years, suffering all the prejudices, whether expressed openly or in a subtle manner. I was analyzing colleagues and friends coming from different countries and wanted to stay in Bergasse at whatever price. I didn't believe that the Nazis would arrive at my door. After Annerl was arrested by the Gestapo, I felt defeated. Now I have been living in London for a year. My colleagues and my sisters almost certainly will be killed by Hitler. Forgive me. I recognize, finally, that if I stayed in Vienna, psychoanalysis would have disappeared—it would come at the hands of the Nazis, or the hands of the communists that certainly will take power. The decision to move to London, while difficult, saved not only the lives of those I love, but also allowed psychoanalytic theory a chance to survive and spread throughout the world. I never disguised my antipathy for the *modus vivendi* of the Americans, but their capacity to transform everything they put their hands on into an object to consume offered my discoveries a chance to gain strength and recognition. They, those Americans, are a type of modern-day Midas.

From my bed I follow the movement of the sun. Night is falling. At night, I feel more apprehensive. I feel little longing for Martha, more for Annerl and Paula. The pain grows, and my daydreams lose all logic. The mosquito netting protects me from the flies but partially obstructs my view of the road. The light dims and lets the twilight enter.

Paula enters still smiling, greets me, now in English, and offers me vegetable soup. I note that despite all her efforts, she stays farther from my lacerated face. She insists on feeding me; and when Annerl enters, I have a spoon in my mouth and am unable to greet her.

After dinner they both leave, and I turn my attention

to the antiques, my old and good gods, to the origin of religions—a theme that never abandons me. Greek gods, Roman or Egyptian—all lined up in a row and observing my suffering. I know I am dying. But how does one defeat death? I can't, except by writing books, though one doesn't know if they will be read in the future. I remember that Nazi phrase that at times has been used against my contributions and those of other Jewish writers: "We are against the glorification of the instincts; we want to restore the nobility of the human soul; thus, we burn the books of Sigmund Freud." I thought that, surely there has been some progress since the burning of witches in the Middle Ages: Now they content themselves with burning books.

It is night and I see someone enter the bedroom. I close my eyes and pretend to nap; at the same time I ask, both in fear and happiness, *more visits?*

Wednesday, September 20, 1939

I awake and again hear the sound of soldiers marching. They follow the command of a loud, harsh voice that yells two syllables close together and barely intelligible. The men understand and follow the orders. I think again about Vienna and admit missing the city where I lived for almost my entire life. In the final analysis, I wish I could continue living in Bergasse. I didn't believe the Nazis would invade my home, but it happened. Now I think I was naïve. They not only came into my living room, but into my kitchen and all the bedrooms. Fortunately, my collection was preserved or simply didn't interest them.

With some effort, I open my eyes and see Anna, Martha, and Paula, then Max. It's morning. I speak before them and—making an effort to speak above a whisper— murmur that I am well and slept all right. We all know that I am lying. I am not hungry; but hoping to fool them, ask for some breakfast. They eye me mistrustfully, and Paula immediately brings a tray; at the same time, they agree to watch my meal without interruption. I swallow. I do it slowly, and once again I cannot taste. I allege my jaw hurts. They accept my apology. As a matter of fact, surprisingly, the pain is better this morning. The three pay no attention to the anti-aircraft guns that sound like they are very near the house. When the plate is half eaten, they leave, whispering something like, "He didn't eat much!" The patrols disappear. I remember my mother, Amalie. I knew that I was her favorite, but I didn't like my siblings' comments, especially my sisters' when they talked about it.

In Vienna I gave up when the Gestapo's provocations became daily events. I was afraid when they summoned me to give evidence and Anna offered herself in my place. When Annerl was interrogated for the entire day, I spent the time pacing back and forth with a cigar in my mouth. At that point, I had to agree with Princess Marie Bonaparte and Ernest Jones and decided to pack the suitcases and the antiquities. I would go to London because I wanted my discoveries to resound throughout the world.

My mother, Amalie, and my name: My birth certificate records my name as Sigismund, a corruption of Schlomo, from the Hebrew Shelomoh, a version of Solomon. Years later, I changed my name to Sigmund. I think about the relationship between my original name and the work I undertook... the things, objects, affects, words, and the language.

Suddenly, a new wave of pain interrupts my thoughts. I question: What would become of human beings without language? Were not the cave paintings, the paintbrush, or the sculptor's chisel also forms of a more sophisticated language? I always concerned myself with language and silences. Both when we speak and when we fall silent, we desire. Years ago, I said that when we speak, we ask something of someone, either in the positive or the negative.

Language, that which we try to say to another, is unsteady ground: My work, *Die Verneinung,* was translated into English as *Negation.* I didn't agree but did not succeed in convin-

Freud, aged sixteen with his mother, Amalie.

cing them that their English title lost subtle distinctions of the German language. I left it alone.

In my musings, I understand that the raw material of psychoanalysis is what people say, where the distinction between objectivity and subjectivity is irrelevant. The human being has a compulsion to classify everything that is. Would this be a defensive act? In language, what is the relationship between words and the things to which they refer?

I look out the window and see the trees losing their leaves. Soon fall will be in full swing, and I will not be in this room or in this world. Pain acts as if it were a drain through which life empties. It is true; it is cyclical, and there is little we can do to change it. Sharp pains throb in my jaw, each more intense than the last. Gangrene is attacking the tissue. It is the end. It is difficult to speak, but still I think. Everything I think amounts to a chronicle of terminal pain. I know it acts as a helpless defense against approaching death.

I think of a short novel by Goethe, titled *The Elective Affinities.* I don't tire of stating that writers and philosophers grasp the infinite expanse of the human soul more rapidly than do the scientists. In this work my favorite writer, Goethe, succeeds in synthesizing everything I say about the human being, his strengths and weaknesses. Without an excess of conceptualizing that makes us short-sighted or unjust, the novel addresses the spectrum of human issues—the reason for closeness and distance between people, the expectations and disappointments, their contradictions and injustices, nobility and villainy. Finally, he synthesizes with rigor and depth, dilemmas that the scientist treats superficially, including my psychoanalytic theory. Am I a writer or a scientist? How can I understand these ideas when death is watching?

Thursday, September 21, 1939

I awake but can't manage to, or don't want to, open my eyes. I feel nostalgia for the pain I felt two days before; it was nothing compared to this morning. I try to hear or guess the movements in the house, of the automobiles and military vehicles that climb and descend Maresfield. The noises sound louder than those I would hear in Bergasse.

At that moment some fingertips stroke my face,

smooth my hair, and with the help of a small cloth, wipe the drops of sweat from my forehead. These caring gestures cause me to keep my eyes closed and, once again, to pretend to sleep. It doesn't work. I open my eyes slowly and see faces. Martha is closest, then Anna, and in the back, Paula. I smile gratefully, though I feel discouraged. Martha's expression is closed, serious, and tired; Anna appears to be making a great effort to act naturally; and Paula, farthest back, appears to be crying. I look at each of them with firmness, trying to transmit safety and strength in the face of what was to come. At the same time, I think about how difficult it is refrain from observing my own behavior and that of others. Maybe it comes from years of dedicated listening to people's complaints and laments and seeking, foremost, to understand what lay between the lines of what they said. More than anything, I value lucidity and fear being at the mercy of outsiders.

I ramble. My life was not useless. I achieved almost all of my dreams and helped people to value what they dreamt, both during the day or during the night. They came from distant pla-

ces to seek me out, trusting that the science I invented would offer the solution to all of their maladies, theirs and humanity's. My hopes were more modest, but I kept silent to preserve the faith of those to whom I listened. My work began with observation of clinical cases in neurology and psychiatry, but soon I would not know what to

Freud and Fliess in 1890.

call my work. Did I abandon medicine or did it abandon me? Years ago I wrote to Fliess and told him that I was not a man of science, not an observer, not even an experimenter or thinker. I considered myself a conqueror or adventurer. In recent times my interests lie in philosophy and literature. At times, I listen to my patients with a secret feeling of desperation. It is horrible to listen and remain quiet. I am, in the end, distant from Claude Bernard and close to Dostoyevsky, far from Descartes and near to Nietzsche. My time has passed.

These digressions help to soften my pain to the extent that is possible. In the book I just finished reading, *The Magic Skin* by Balzac, many passages reminded me of my own books. Balzac compares life to a game and in the beginning says ironically that when we enter a casino, we begin by losing the hat that we hang on the hat rack. Man drains himself through two instinctual acts, which prevent full existence and lead to death: To want and to master. These do not bring wisdom, which is the natural culmination of wanting or *knowing*. Glory is a poor alternative; and in addition to everything else, it's expensive: The happiness it brings does not last; it consumes our strength or results in disgrace that erases our virtues.

Balzac, Balzac, you and the other writers say everything that I sought to say and couldn't. Rafael, in few words your character says that in life every time we desire, we travel in the direction of death. It is true. We have little awareness of our movement toward death. The idea is a movement, and immense energy. Man doesn't invent energies. Even God can be a form of movement. In suicide there is something grandiose: When a man falls, no doubt it is a great downfall. I feel hungry, but I can't satisfy it, to swallow without unleashing the pain, each time more piercing.

I looked around, the billowing curtains of the bedroom/ office refresh my sweaty body. I wanted to face death between the curtains, watching. I slept again and dreamt about a train trip. Death was as near as Dover.

Paula approaches and tries again to make me swallow some broth. I feel revulsion and nausea. I take advantage of her proximity and whisper in a hiss: "Call Max, please!" She leaves hurriedly and Max enters immediately. I ask everyone leave the room, except my doctor, my friend.

"Max, naturally you know my son, Oliver, do you not?"

"Certainly, Professor!"

"Well, then, his name is due to the English writer and politician, Oliver Cromwell, who I read in my youth. Cromwell said: "I was not given to drink or sleep simply to hurry the hour of my departure.""

"Dear Professor, I think you have always inquired about death."

"Certainly, Max, more all the time. You don't think it ought to be on my mind? Especially these days?"

Max looks worried. Smiling, I ask in a whisper if he has yet read *The Magic Skin*. He said that he has not yet. I say that it is a novel quite similar to *Faust* and deals with obtaining all of life's pleasures in exchange for immortality: Always a man faces his death and eternity. *Now, Max, I ought to say I read very little, wrote a great deal, confused colleagues with friends; and friends, with colleagues. The book speaks of something that is happening to me: All of Raphael's desires are satisfied, but each satisfaction makes his Magic Skin shrink. We are diminished in size when we desire a lot. It is true of me.*

"Max, listen to me carefully. Many years ago, in 1929, if I remember right, you promised that when I determined that nothing more remained of my life except torture, you would help me. The hour has arrived."

He responded with a shake of the head and wet eyes. He remembered. He held my hand for some moments and squeezed it. He could not hold back the tears. He stood up, picked up a valise and took out a hypodermic syringe and a full vial of morphine. He automatically punctured the cover with a small needle, pulled the piston, and put two centigrams of morphine in the syringe. He looked at me, and I said, "Be sure to tell Annerl, but I don't want her to watch."

Max Schur.

I felt a small prick, and then I was taken by immense pleasure that there was much I would not feel. My respiration, uncomfortable and panting, rapid, ineffective and superficial, gave way to a great relief. A warm feeling ran through my body; and, at the same time, I felt a light, pleasant dizziness... my skin, previously cold, warmed up... my breathing, previously superficial, slowed and paused, my heart began to beat regularly, the sweat disappeared; the uncomfortable gasses, also. I began to see lights and have visual and auditory sensations. Nothing bothered me any longer.

The voices sounded far away. I felt an irresistible need to sleep. Before closing my eyes, I looked at Max, tried to move my head in a sign of gratitude. The curtains and the mosquito netting moved. I sensed death. Irony continues to be part of life.

I looked in the direction of death and murmured,

"See, I took all the measures before you got here. Heads, I win; tails, you lose."

BERGASSE 19 CLOSES ITS DOORS

I never had the habit of listening to the radio, but during these times all of us felt curious and concerned about the destiny of Austria. Over the radio, I heard commentaries and propaganda that Adolf Hitler would successfully annex Austria to Germany and thus, among other things, eliminate the last remnants of the Austro-Hungarian Empire. I checked the calendar after hearing the news: March 13, 1938. I saw

the time on my watch and automatically wound it, much like I had for many years. I noticed that my primitive rancor for Austria would end, to be substituted by a useless feeling of gratitude: I knew that this country where I lived all my life never would be the same. The news also said that Hitler would make a friendly "visit" to the country after the annexation on March 14.

Adolf Hitler made Austrian minister, Kurt von Schuschnigg, leave the government and in his place inserted Seyss-Inquart. During the month of February, I wrote to Max Eitingon and left off reading the papers that increasingly lied. I said to him, "You read that the Jews of Germany are prohibited from giving German names to their children? They can only respond by requiring the Nazis to abstain from using the popular names John, Joseph, and Mary. Schuschnigg's best intentions toward the Jews would only be respected when he was divested of any authority. This time will be short. After his removal, all that remains is to wait."

I thought that my exit from Vienna would bring about the immediate destruction of the group of people interested in psychoanalysis. But, if it was not possible to avoid the annexation of Austria to Germany, it still was possible to prevent the annexation of psychoanalytic theory to Nazi ideology through the acceptance of Hitler's censorship. In peaceful Austria, Nazism found fertile soil for its ideas, much more than in Germany itself: The powerful Catholic Church took the curious and provocative position of agreeing to hoist the Nazi flag in their churchyards.

The events which took place in Vienna completely supported my point of view: The Viennese citizens—who before the invasion behaved in a peaceful, serene, gracious manner—suddenly acted as agents of physical and psychological violence—attacking, humiliating, and killing Jews with more relish than their friends and colleagues, the Nazis. I always said it was not completely correct to say that the human being is socialized. I prefer to say that he is domesticated like a dog and, at the same time, never completely trustworthy like the dog is.

It was March, and I wrote to my son, Ernst, telling him that we were waiting for the "green light" from the income tax so we could travel to England. I told him, also, that it was the time for the Wandering Jew to rest someplace. I revealed my fear in relation to my collection of antiquities and, in a self--critical tone, closed by comparing myself to a man who tries to save a bird cage from a burning house.

***

I was writing the letter in my office when I heard strong, insistent banging on the front door. I stood up; and when I arrived at the living room, I came across a group of youths dressed in brown uniforms with armbands exhibiting a swastika, the symbol used by Buddhists to signify happiness. They acted like soldiers, were armed and visibly nervous. One of them, despite seeming to be the most arrogant of them, appeared no more than fifteen years of age. Speaking with the speed of people who obeyed orders automatically, they began to search the house without anyone's permission and from time to time asked where the money was. Martha asked them calmly if they would like to sit down because she would like to treat them courteously. The invaders did not respond.

After finding the money, which they alleged to be little, they gave us a receipt. I knew I had no money left; I accepted the receipt and said that never in my life had I paid so much for a visit. The event that scared me, though, was when they seized Anna and took her to be interrogated. In truth, I wanted to go with them, but Anna offered to go alone, alleging that my health was not good. Surprisingly, they accepted a statement signed by Hans Pichler that my health was precarious. On the same day, they also confiscated the entire family's passports.

Distressed, I returned to the office, paced back and

forth, worried about Annerl, and smoked one cigar after another, despite knowing the evils caused by smoking. Max entered the office and, one more time, alerted me to the damage caused by tobacco. I responded that the cigar had kept me company since my youth and helped me face life, not to mention that it increased my ability to work and enhanced my self-control. Despite this, the damages had already been done. Later, I learned that Max had given Anna capsules of cyanide that she could use in case the interrogation exceeded her physical and moral resistance.

I waited the entire day for news. Late in the afternoon, Anna returned home, visibly exhausted by the intense interrogation. At the moment when I looked at my daughter from head to toe, I finally decided to leave Austria.

***

I had written a letter to Ernest Jones in which I sought to convince him and other friends that I didn't feel like having any birthday celebration; despite this, it appeared that my exile to England was becoming inevitable. In that same letter, I informed Jones that Princess Marie should arrive in Vienna at the beginning of the week to accompany us to Paris if we were liberated by the Nazi authorities. I concluded by saying that I was discouraged, preferring to be in better health; and I remembered the French proverb: "If you are bound to lose, it's not worth playing."

***

I was in the office on that Sunday, reliving the fear that

Anna's arrest caused me. At the same time, I re-read some essays by Thomas Macaulay, the politician and author whom I had appreciated for a long time. In truth, I strongly identified with his liberal way of thinking and his personal ambition. Macaulay received an excellent education at Trinity College, Cambridge. One other memory was that he fought for the emancipation of the Jews. A re-reading showed, once again, that a second reading is always most profound and instructive: We end up noticing unsuspected details.

Freud's committee in 1902. Seated: Freud, Sandor Ferenczi, and Hanns Sachs. Standing: Otto Rank, Karl Abraham, Max Eitingon, and Ernest Jones.

Reflecting on the annexation of Austria by Germany, I considered it sad that an empire that had controlled and governed dozens of nations was now so limited in his territory and in its political sovereignty. The rulers of Austria had become mediocre and fearful, the country was increasingly diminished from its splendor at the end of the century.

I was immersed in these reflections when I heard a light knock at the door. Anna entered anxiously and told me that various members of the Psychoanalytic Society of Vienna were for reasons of security meeting in the living room and invited me to the extraordinary session. They had opted to meet at Bergasse 19, and not the headquarters at Bergasse 7. Anna also told me that she wanted me to preside over the meeting.

Surprised, but only a little, I got up slowly and went to the living room. The turnout was low. Annerl told me that the meeting had but one item on the agenda: To assess the Society's continued viability in Vienna. After I took a seat, Anna informed me that the Society had received a communication from Berlin saying that Dr. Carl Müeller-Braunschweig was in transit to Vienna, accompanied by a German official, to assume the direction of the Society. The letter said that in addition to integrating various treatment techniques into psychoanalytic theory, Müeller-Braunschweig intended to Arianize psychoanalysis, an idea which simultaneously aroused fear and laughter among the members since the only non-Jewish psychoanalyst present was Richard Sterba. That observation facilitated the next step of the meeting, the unanimous self-dissolution of the Society. I looked at Sterba and asked what he thought of the decision. He told me he agreed, not only with the result of the vote, but he personally thought that psychoanalytic theory engendered a liberating profession and that its submission to the Nazi regulation would make no sense. Sterba added that he would also leave Austria with his entire family.

I took a deep breath and secretly lamented that things had come to this. At this moment I reminded them that when General Tito destroyed the Temple of Jerusalem, Rabbi Yochanan ben Zakkai asked permission to transform his school in Yavneh into a center for the study of the Torah. And I concluded that psychoanalysis and its students will have to do the same.

Following this statement, someone suggested that from that day—March 13, 1938—the seat of the study, thought, and theory formation of psychoanalysis would be wherever I was. All agreed, and thus psychoanalysis closed its activities in Vienna. I could not imagine if and when it would again be studied in that country.

***

Vienna IX, Bergasse 19, 03/23/1938

Annerl,

I always end up thinking that my skill in writing is grea-ter than my skill in speaking. Currently, I better understand my difficulty speaking since my illness makes it more and more dif-ficult all the time. This letter is written under the effects of strong emotions, considering recent events. Your detention for a day convinced me that, sadly, we have no place in Austria. I could not tolerate your absence for so many hours, and I came to un-derstand Max's reason for giving you the capsules of cyanide. Simply imagining your being hurt caused me immense revul-sion.

When I saw you enter the house at night, I felt a mix of concern and relief; at the same time, I made the decision I had been postponing, that we should leave this country where the climate is increasingly infused with anti-Semitism. From now on we will do everything possible to go together, preferably to England. I am certain that we will not have to submit to any type of humiliation there.

But I also write this letter for other reasons, to say some things that maybe never have been said, probably because I considered them self-evident.

When your mother, Martha, got pregnant for the sixth time, I must say I was horrified. How to sustain a family so big and maintain ones dignity? I corresponded by letter with my then friend, Fliess, about his research on contraceptives. How welcome they would be!

The years passed and you were gaining more and more importance in the family's heart, at the same time you became my right hand in research. It was difficult to separate my dear daughter from the work companion. Your siblings left and your mother never made secret her lack of interest in things psychoanalytic.

During the time left to me, I sometimes ask myself about the fact that you have not married. You know, as do I, that you had various suitors, but I feared your leaving and never considered them to be at your level. Eventually colleagues suggested that, in truth, I didn't consider them to be at my level. Who knows?

With regard to the spread of psychoanalytic theory, I was certain you could do a better job than anyone else. From the technical or theoretical point of view, maybe it was possible to find someone who could advance the theory; but your loyalty to me and the theory would safeguard what I created.

Without any doubt, my gratitude makes me think about you in a different way than your siblings—with the exception of Martin, who dedicated himself to publishing our work. The others set their own goals and left. I am not complaining. Or am I?

I repeat that your interrogation motivated me to leave Austria. I always sought to maintain self-control and couldn't do it during the time I waited for you. Your return signaled that we

*ought to begin a new life with total freedom and with a guaran-
tee of the minimal conditions necessary to continue my work.
Only forty-three years old, you have your whole life in front of
you and certainly can count on the support of friends who are
with us and are accompanying us into exile. During the time
remaining, if some does remain to me, I intend to write at least
three letters to people who affected my life and to whom I owe
gratitude. It goes without saying that this is the first. Possibly,
many friends and colleagues will be left out, but my physical
condition is deteriorating more rapidly than I anticipated.*

*In case we can locate in London, I would like to ask you
to maintain some distance from Melanie Klein, whose ideas fail
to abide by the principles of the theory I created. I do not like the
possibility that the theory might take on a political or sectarian
coloration. All of my life I sought to follow a rational course and
now fear that my ideas might be reduced to simply one more
of the dozens conceptions of the psyche that exist everywhere. I
feel that Mrs. Klein looks for points of disagreement and doesn't
pay attention to the similarities that exist in our points of view.
By the way, I have come to think that our coming to England
displeases her, and I don't know if I would like to be mistaken.*

*I would like you to maintain a close friendship with
Dorothy and with Princess Marie. Our years of contact have
convinced me that they are sincere and loyal friends. Keep your
eye on our friend, Ernest Jones. At times I think that though
his investment is intense, it focuses more on political aspects
of psychoanalysis than personal ties. Maybe I am being unfair,
and this time I would like to be wrong. I am only trying to be
honest about my feelings, and this honesty has over my long life
cost me many friends. In relation to some, time showed that my
suspicions were correct, whereas with other friends, unhappily, I
lost them in the course of an intemperate evaluation.*

To close, Annerl, go forward and begin from this day to

live with my absence. They will all need you.

Affectionately,
Your Poppa

***

Princess Marie Bonaparte with her dog.

Finally, after interventions by friends, especially the Princess and, later, the American ambassador in France, William Bullitt, our passports were returned. I looked at the documents and noted that they were not the same as those confiscated. The new passports were issued by the Reich and bore a swastika.

On the same day I observed that my neighbors' windows were decorated with flags bearing a swastika in the center. Austria had undeniably accepted its annexation with pride. I concluded that my presence on that street in Vienna or anywhere in Austria was impossible and unwelcome.

The comings and goings in relationship to travel were, in a way, expected. It occurred to me that bureaucracy was one of the beloved offspring of paranoia. The Gestapo did not release the *Unbedenklichkeitserklärung* until the beginning of June. Together with the permission to travel, I received a letter declaring that I had been treated well by the Gestapo. I asked to borrow a pen from one of the soldier and signed on the table while telling them that, if possible, I would like to add some words in my own hand to the letter. So, I wrote that no one could doubt that I had been well treated by the Gestapo and that I would recommend it to everyone. The "authorities" did not understand my provocative sarcasm, fortunately.

My worry from then on was to insure that my collection of antiques was properly packed. I still sought information concerning the liberation of my sisters. One Gestapo had rudely advised the Princess that this would be difficult. She told me that the invaders' arrogance diminished her political influence.

Finally, on Saturday, June 4, Martha, Anna, Dr. Stross, Paula, Lün, and I caught two taxis on Bergasse and asked them to take us about five kilometers to Westbahnhof. I got in the taxi and for the last time in my life looked upon the building where I had worked for many decades. Riding through the streets of Vienna, I passed houses and shops with swastikas in the windows. Vienna had adopted a completely new conception of man, race, and politics. Most appeared to burst with pride at the display of the Nazi flag.

Many friends thought I had underestimated the risks of staying in the city. I always disagreed. On the way to the railroad station, I remembered Hitler's messianic words from the past summer and knew that truly I had been wrong in my evaluation of Hitler and his generals. In a speech which I will never forget, he said, "When I look back five years, I can say it was not the work of human hands only. It is a miracle of the age that you have found me among many millions. And I found you, that is the good fortune of Germany. I will not act. I will wait, no matter what happens. But if you speak, then I will know the time has come to act." The daydream, or the memory, brought a frightening realization: Now I believe!

We reached the train station a little before 3:00 p.m. with the intent to embark on the Orient Express, proceeding

Vilma Kovacs, Dorothy Burlingham and Anna Freud. Photo: Edward Bibring.

through Istanbul toward Paris. Unhappily, I could not count on the company of Princess Marie for the length of the trip. She would wait for us in Paris. My sister-in-law, Minna, who had obtained a visa to leave the previous month, went to Switzerland with Dorothy Burlingham and would arrive in London at the same time.

There was a crowd in the courtyard of the railroad station; and when we got out of the taxi, I noticed that people were curious and watched me, some with a look of admiration, others with disdain. Having difficulty walking and supporting myself on the cane, I felt relieved to spot the train, but it was surrounded by people who clearly were not there to board the train. Without my noticing from whence they came, some of them passed in front of me and formed a human corridor through which I passed, walking as fast as I could looking straight ahead. When I saw the door to the lobby open in front of us and with but a small stair-step, my legs shook for the first time in innumerable journeys by train. I was overcome, knowing that I would never again set foot on Austrian soil.

Two cabins were reserved for my family. The first accommodated Martha, Anna, Lün—a chow on a leash—and myself; the second housed Dr. Josephine Stross and Paula. We sat in the Vienna station only a few minutes; but in situations like that, the wait seemed like forever.

At exactly 3:25 the train began to move. With the cabin curtains down, I could not breathe as easily as I had imagined. Ahead we would still have to face the station at Salzburg and at Munich, home to the Dachau concentration camp. After leaving, Anna told me that we were being discretely accompanied by a staff member of the American embassy that should provide help in case something went wrong.

En route through Austrian territory and then Germany, I had no desire to speak. An apprehensive, suspenseful silence reigned in the cabin. A few minutes before 4:00 in the morning on Sunday, I noticed the train slow down for a stop. I imagined a routine stop; but, at the same time, I knew we were still in Germany.

The train stopped; and through the curtains I saw a group of soldiers in German uniforms. They spoke in loud voices which allowed me to understand the key points. The train slowly regained speed and crossed the Kehl Bridge spanning the Rhine. It stopped soon thereafter, and one more time I caught a glimpse of soldiers, now with red, white, and blue uniforms. Someone knocked on the cabin door. Anna rose and opened it. A French soldier entered and asked to see our passports. He carefully looked at each page, looked at us, said something in French, which I had no interest in understanding, welcomed us and left. He did the same thing at the next cabin.

The train resumed its progress and crossed the border. At that moment, I could again breathe normally and said, in a loud voice for the first time in the last twelve hours, "We are free!"

***

My writing career, at times hesitant, began with *The Interpretation of Dreams*, my classic work—to which I gave the nickname *The Egyptian Book of Dreams*—in which for more than five hundred pages I examined my own dreams and analyzed them as deeply as possible—everything more or less related to death, especially the death of my father. In *Moses and Monotheism,* one of my last books, I focused also on the "death" of Moses. Death, always death.

For years I cultivated a secret admiration for Arthur Schnitzler, an Austrian writer that I considered my "double" and who in his novellas unveiled facts about the human psyche that took me years to understand, and never well enough. Some time before my diagnosis of carcinoma of the palate, I wrote him a letter in which I said, "Your interest in unconscious truths and in instinctual human impulses, your analyses of the dogma at the source of our conventions and culture, your persistence about the polarity of love and death—all of this moved me with a disquieting feeling of familiarity that creates the impression that you already knew through intuition—or by virtue of detailed observation—everything I discovered through laborious work with people."

As a writer's apprentice, I state that many times I almost always constructed complementary lines of thought—for example, the texts about psychoanalytic theory, in which I seek to employ scientific rigor, and the letters directed to friends and collegial confidants. In the second case, I discover in myself a poet who, liberated from the constrictions and conventions of science, gives free run to the creative imagination, to the emotions and cogitations, lending to the text the greatest elegance possible. In my technical works I seek coherency or academic consistency. My letters, on the one hand, and the technical texts, on the other, combine to make me human—who experiences his feelings intensely—and reveal the scientist who employs his method much like the artist uses a chisel.

In life, I chose many correspondents. The intense exchange of letters established a type of dialectic; I had the opportunity to expound on ideas and submit them to someone whom I admired or whom I respected intellectually. It all began in a systematic way with Wilhelm Fliess, when in my first writings I tried to initiate a "Project for a Scientific Psychology." This habit hangs on.

***

After crossing the border, I slept. I dreamt that I was running to catch a train; but when I arrived at the station, it had already left. I awoke, tired and anxious. I thought about the contradiction between my dream and the voyage that I was taking: I wrote somewhere that in a dream "to miss the train" would signify a preoccupation with death, and I should admit that at least on that one night, the train represented, at the minimum, the prolongation of life.

On Sunday morning, June 5, we arrived in Paris—a city for which I harbor a special affection. After graduating from medical school, I was awarded a scholarship by Doctor and Professor Charcot; and from his research, teaching, and thoughts about hypnotism, I learned something that I had an opportunity to repeat many times throughout my life: We are not kings of our own castles.

After the period in which I visited Salpêtrière, I never again considered myself a doctor, at least not a doctor who believes that all human suffering originates from the body. The

Freud and Anna arrive at Gare de L'Est, in Paris.

soul is home to inevitable contradictions, which remain largely unknown to us and affect daily life more than we would be able to tolerate or desire if we were consciously aware of them. Later on, I discovered that those contradictions, beyond their ineffable nature, invent new worlds and that these inventions require and deserve our consideration: They come into existence and ought to be heard, not confronted by logic—a job that in no way resembles the confrontation perpetrated by police.

Princess Marie Bonaparte, William Bullitt, and my son, Ernst, awaited us at Paris' East Station. In addition to these friends, there was a great number of journalists: the Princess and Bullitt, beyond clearly having helped with my escape, were also seeking to make journalists aware that it had happened, with the political goal of increasing international pressure to aid in the liberation of other Jews. Immediately after disembarking, we got into two cars a great deal more comfortable than those in Vienna. The schedule dictated we would rest in Princess Marie's mansion and continue the voyage to Calais at night. After crossing the English Channel on a ferry--boat, we would dock at Dover, England.

The Princess was visibly satisfied. She acted like someone who had accomplished a heroic feat; and at the same time, her gestures and words always expressed gratitude, not just toward me, but toward my entire family, including Paula. Her hospitality was unforgettable. We stayed there for twelve hours.

We crossed the English Channel at night. The sea remained calm, as did my soul. At dawn we arrived in Dover. I couldn't help smelling the strong odor of the sea when the ferry-boat dropped anchor. Now only a short path separated me from my new home. At nineteen years of age, I had visited England for the first time, and I fell in love with the country and its traditions; at that age, I was impressed by the anti-monarchical ideas of Oliver Cromwell, who was also in favor of the full acceptance of Jews on English soil.

When I submitted my documents at the border, I was told that my baggage was not subject to routine inspection since it was considered diplomatic. In truth, from the beginning of my departure from Vienna, I received favors and attention that I never could have imagined, whose origins I was not able to discern.

LONDON

As the train began to move, the speed made me feel free. Victoria Station would be the last stop. As we approached London, the sky looked surprisingly clear, and I knew that rain was forecast only for the regions to the north and east. The passage of the train through the suburbs of the capital brought memories of my adolescence and made me nostalgic. Finally, the train began to reduce speed; and in the distance I glimpsed the turn-of-the-century design of the station's east terminal. I knew this smooth coordination of boat and rail transport would no longer be possible once armed conflict began.

We arrived in London in late morning on June 6, 1938, a sunny Sunday. My mood was as bright as the sunshine. The rail company changed our disembarkation platform at the last minute in order to avoid a large crowd that had gathered to watch the arrival of the exiled creator of psychoanalysis. When I stepped down from the car behind my companions, I looked up at the station's thirty-meter ceiling and admired its height and the compound glass skylights. English-style columns supported the roof, and pigeons flew to and fro below its immense shelter. The birds felt protected in their home.

Within the crowd boarding and disembarking the rail car stood our welcoming committee: my children, Mathilde and Martin, and Ernest Jones and his wife. My emotions grew

Mathilde, Freud, Jones, and Lucie Freud

still stronger, and I could see its reflection in the eyes of these beloved people.

I accompanied them to the station entrance where we found three taxis parked with their doors open. Martha, Ernest, his wife, and I took seats in the first car. Anna, Dr. Stross, Mathilde, Martin, Paula, Lün, and the luggage filled the second and third vehicles.

Ernest Jones informed us that our temporary home was situated at #139 Elsworthy Rd. in an extremely pleasant, residential region in the north of London, near the Primrose Hill Park. He suggested a little site-seeing on the way. At that moment I didn't know if my fatigue was mental or physical, but I agreed.

Immediately after leaving Victoria Station we reached Buckingham Palace, official residence of King George VI, then to #10 Downing St., where Prime Minister Neville Chamberlain was possibly coordinating intense diplomatic negotiations that, as we learned later, proved to be a failure. We crossed the famous Trafalgar Square and took a long look at the National Gallery, a place I certainly intended to visit more than once if my health permitted. We turned to Piccadilly Circus, took Regent Street, and crossed Regent's Park. The neighborhood appeared typically English, surrounded by beautifully landscaped lawns. To my gratitude the cars finally stopped in front of our new home. Without a doubt, the beautiful and comfortable house would make me forget the old Bergasse house.

Eager to write and describe my experiences but still without my own stationery, I decided to inform some people of our new address. In my first letter from Elsworthy, I wrote to my old friend and colleague, Max Eitingon, who had also left Berlin and now resided in Jerusalem. Full of good news, I wrote about how Princess Marie Bonaparte received us in Paris, the memorable day in her home, and especially my arrival in London for the third and final time in my life. I felt discouraged by Minna's continued illness. At the end of the letter, I confessed to Eitingon that I preferred to relate more or less trivial information because "the emotional climate these days is difficult to understand, almost indescribable. I feel triumphant to have escaped, but my freedom pains me because I loved my prison. My enchantment with a new environment (that makes us want to shout, "Heil Hitler!") is mixed with irritation caused by the small oddities of a strange environment. The happy celebrations of a new life are muted by this question: How long can a tired heart continue to beat?"

Curiously, as soon as I got to Elsworthy, a letter arrived from Mrs. Melanie Klein. She missed my arrival in London and said that we would meet soon. I responded immediately. The meeting never took place.

***

England's somber mood after Germany's annexation of Austria stood in stark contrast to Austria's euphoria. Hitler approached leadership in a completely different way than England's government under Churchill. Hitler and his advisor's orchestrated a theatrical self-promotion, while his

English counterpart retained his British reserve in a call to battle which captured the hearts and souls and of the citizenry. Both made use of rhetoric; but while Hitler hypnotized the crowds with his hysteria and studied, exaggerated gestures, Churchill rose above pure narcissism and soberly reminded the British of the values which made the survival of Great Britain and its people necessary. Hitler's speaking style, decisive and inflammatory, focused on him. He spoke of himself and his personal ambition; the German people came second. The words of Churchill referred to the people who were listening. He sought to protect the nation, not harm others.

When Hitler came to power, he was in the habit of saying that tobacco was the American Indian's revenge against the Whites for having introduced them to alcohol. In this way, he justified the prejudice that caused him to prohibit the use of cigarettes by soldiers in public places, arguing that the physical harm caused by smoke weakened the Arian race. Meanwhile, he encouraged the distribution of free cigarettes in certain places—ghettos, for example—to any non-Arians who wanted them.

***

As I was beginning my discoveries, I published an article which was translated by James Strachey with the title, *Screen Memories*. The work treated the way information is retained in memory. More recently, I have noticed that my colleagues tend to consider the more remote memories of the past to serve a defensive function, as if a current memory acts like a type of camouflage for real events and a coherent narrative were defensively hiding true past events.

I now consider that view mistaken. It is reminiscent

of an archeological model, one on which I did, in fact, base it. In reviewing my position, I propose we change that view and give up the mechanistic illusion that at some moment we can recover the "original" facts deposited in the psyche. I dare say that it is a mistake to catapult the significant events of our existence into the past, present, or future. These temporal distinctions end up creating problems during an analysis because they place epistemological questions before the psychoanalytic work and in the end don't contribute anything to understanding the analysand's mind.

The psyche, especially in reference to the Unconscious, does not pay attention to the calendar or the human clock. Other demands organize psychological events. The Unconscious may organize itself along spatial and temporal dimensions. The words making up the patient's narrative are naturally uttered in the present even though they supposedly refer to, and to some extent, reinvent the past or an imagined future more or less remote. The presence of the temporal and/ or spatial dimension in the narrative is obviously tied to the fragment of a significant past event. No matter what form it takes, the only event—having "occurred" in the past, present, or future—appears in the narrative; and it seeks only to attend to the speaker's desires. Nothing more.

Thus, there is no criterion that would allow the analyst to distinguish which heard fragments are "true" from those that merely function as disguise. The evidence for this distinction must come from the speaker. When the analyst insists on the correctness of his interpretation at all costs, he indulges in what I previously called wild analysis, that is, interpretations fueled by preconceived theories, beliefs, and values presented by an authority figure who presents himself as the "owner of knowledge."

***

Fatigue defeated me, and I went to slept. The bed surprised me. It was immeasurably more comfortable that the train's bunk. I slept without even eating. I awoke to June 7 and, to my surprise, Paula had already brought in the newspapers. They all warmly reported my arrival in London. *The Times* noted that sixty-two years after first visiting, Professor Sigmund Freud arrived in London from Paris yesterday and from that date would reside in London. It even said that I had lived eighty-two years and arrived with my wife, Martha, my daughter and principal collaborator, Anna, and my son, Martin, lawyer and editor of the International Psychoanalytic Publishing House, which was recently interdicted by the Germans. My children, Mathilde and Ernst, had already moved to England. The newspaper also affirmed that "Professor Freud, 'abandoned his entire estate,' leaving it to the Austrian authorities and the Nazis. He received help from various friends and colleagues in obtaining an exit visa from the country and brought with him books and a collection of antique art pieces that he considered his greatest fortune."

Anna controlled my schedule, and she made room for me to receive important people. Many times I felt great anticipation and pleasure to receive them; other times, not so much. Soon I noted that most of the visitors did not come from psychoanalytic circles; they were intellectuals, artists, and writers who had no interest in the science of psychoanalysis. Among those visitors, I had the pleasure of a long conversation with H. G. Wells, the great English writer, whom I had previously met.

Our first days in London were almost festive, filled with a swell of optimism, but I always sought to maintain a critical eye and a clear head. I wrote to my brother, telling him of the homage that I was receiving, coming from all directions and from very different people. My welcome almost always came with by fruit and confections. Some letters suggested that I might cease to be a non-believer, because my liberation was, in fact, proof of a miracle. I concluded my letter to Alexander by saying that late in life I was for the first time feeling famous.

On June 23 representatives of the Royal British Society came to my house with a book in which they registered the names of illustrious members. Such a visit is the exclusive prerogative of monarchs, and they came to collect my signature as an honorary member. I confirmed that the book bore the signatures of Isaac Newton and Charles Darwin. Needless to say, this greatly fueled my vanity. The signing ceremony was witnessed by my daughter, Anna, and by Princess Marie Bonaparte who even filmed the event.

If I remember correctly, in this month Ernst acquired the house at #20 Maresfield Gardens and started remodeling it. It was also situated in the north of London, where I would spend my final days. I did not talk to people about my failing health, despite the likelihood that everyone was thinking the same thing. It contained one more irony: I, Sigmund Freud, knew that one should not talk about the topic and didn't even want to. It showed me that sometimes it is better to say little or nothing at all.

The other visitor I received during these days was my friend, Stefan Zweig, accompanied by the ostentatious painter, Salvador Dali, his wife Gala, and a certain millionaire. The following day, I wrote to Zweig to thank him for the visit. In the letter I told him that I thought the surrealists had come to consider me a patron saint. I confess I had a prejudice with regard to the surrealists, but my contact with Dali made me reconsider my opinion. The other visitor was said to be a candidate for analysis. He told Zweig that anyone's intentions to undergo analysis should be tested— as if psychoanalysis were a woman who wants to be seduced, but knows that she will not be considered worthy unless she displays some resistance.

After establishing my residency in London, I thought it prudent to change my will. Thus, at the end to July, 1938, in addition to some details of minor importance and despite perceiving some dissatisfaction on Anna's part, I willed the copyrights of all my books to my grandchildren. My collection of antiquities and by library would remain Anna's. I think that due to her increasingly intense emotional and intellectual proximity, she naturally felt deserving of more rights.

***

During the month of September, the remodeling of our future residence in Maresfield Gardens was being completed, so we left Elsworthy and became temporary guests in a small hotel called the Esplanade, located at #2 Warrington Crescent in Maida Vale. Access to the hotel was easy. We simply took the stairs down to the Warwick Avenue metro station. Considering my physical weakness, Anna hired a taxi. When we arrived, I stood outside a few minutes, observing the facade while supported by my cane and talked with Anna about the comfort of the accommodations and the quality of English food. I had been forewarned about the tastelessness of English cooking.

We were talking when, curiously, Anna told me that the hotel had a diversified history. It had been constructed in 1865; and in 1880, was transformed into a school of home economics for young women. Some years later it was converted into a maternity hospital and maintained by the Methodist

Church. The first elevator in London was installed in the building; and finally, Anna told me that in 1912 a famous, brilliant mathematician named Alan Turing was born in that building and in a matter of days would be arriving from the United States to help the British Government decipher the cryptography used by the Germans in transmission of their coded messages. Anna completed her report, saying that Turing and I had in common the job of deciphering codes or enigmas. I responded that this aspect in common was superficial: the enigmas that always concerned me are not palpable and many times my translations—if I have them—offer many faces or interpretations, while Turing's were objective, his deciphering aiming at winning wars. The wars that occupied me were intimate, its battlefields located on the subjective landscape.

I stayed in that hotel for several days during the month of September, and I remember that I occupied room 17. The other unforgettable fact was that during these months, Dr. Pichler came from Vienna, performed another surgery, and returned to Austria on the following day. The procedure was radical, and the exams revealed that the lesions were undoubtedly cancerous. From then on, it became progressively difficult to eat, smoke, and talk.

On September 16, the remodeling of Maresfield Gardens was finally concluded. Martha and Paula moved there at the same time that Hitler and Mussolini met in Munich and decided to conquer the world. Minna joined us, and began her slow and painful recovery. When I walked into the house at Maresfield Gardens on September 27, I again imitated a Nazi salute, provoking fear and then laughter. Everyone understood I was celebrating our freedom, thanks to Adolf Hitler.

20, Maresfield Gardens, London, N.W.3
10/2/1938

My beloved and severe Princess,

As you will surely see, the words that follow come in the form of a letter like those I wrote to you many years ago. But I should tell you that I do not intend to exchange information, not even to send news, since we are living under the same roof, as we have since our wedding. I take advantage of the time in which I am not seeing patients or studying life to write a declaration of love, so to speak. I seek to look back at our life and of the events that brought us together and, at times, to distance us from one another.

There is no secret that I am living out my last days and benefit from the almost-silent dedication of each person in the house. Throughout my life, I have dedicated myself to writing and responding to letters. I admit that my habit grew stronger during our engagement while you were in Hamburg and I lived in Paris.

This letter intends to outline the events of our shared life. I distinctly remember that at the beginning, our letters were passionate. From the day we first met each other until we got married, I must have written more than a hundred letters; many events happened, many pains and pleasures were shared. Now we are living together, along with Minna, and are unhappily watching the deterioration of her health.

I would like to record the first events that brought us together. Your staying in Hamburg, while it may have made it easier for us to exchange letters and become increasingly intimate, it also made me aware that your mother was counting on the distance leading to our break-up. My persistence produced a large number of letters that, I now better understand, prevented us from growing apart. Our engagement gave me confidence in your commitment. During the engagement and through the letters, I made many promises and plans. Later, I admit, I did not fulfill many of the promises I made.

I understand that your mother did not look kindly on our union. Considering your father's story, his success and weaknesses, it would be natural for her to want her daughter to find someone who would guarantee her a better life, more comfort, and some degree of social acceptance in an environment that everyone knew was hostile to the less fortunate and especially to the Jews. My professional life and scientific pursuits resulted from a monumental effort to overcome the barriers that confronted to me, sometimes very clearly, sometimes in a veiled form.

My declarations of love bordered on irritation. I asked too much, whereas your demonstrations were restrained. In those days, I imagined that your love for me was "less" than my love for you. Now I know that when I insisted in declaring my love, I was anxiously hoping that in the next letter you would do the same, and with the same intensity. Do you remember how often I said I had a talent for provoking your resistance, how we always fought, and you never gave in? We were two people who were different in every detail of life and, despite this, decided to love each other. During that time, I noticed that you rarely took my side and eventually said that I had no influence over your life. It was painful to hear this truth back then. After half a century, I know that your approach was stronger and more realistic. Staying in Hamburg, you challenged me and made me prove my love.

Later, I studied with Master Charcot in Paris. I had decided to learn the maximum in a minimal amount of time and return to have you once and for all. I did not succeed in living a full life in the City of Light. In the time available for leisure, I de-

dicated myself to writing letters—to you, principally—and used pinches of cocaine. At some parties or meetings at the homes of professors, I felt the atmosphere to be intolerable, and at such times the cocaine was a great help.

While I studied, I focused on professional conquests through the creation of a new method for the treatment of neurotics. At the same time, I sought to save money to make our marriage possible.

Remember when I suggested you read Don Quixote? *I insisted on reading it in Spanish. My appetite for learning languages was a reflection of my ambition. I dreamed of being recognized on every continent. I could not stop seeing Dulcinea in you, relying on the idea that you would be at my side. My worries reached my body, even to the point of hiding my myocarditis from you, so as to not worry you.*

After awhile, I experienced a lowering of libido and had little sexual interest. Even so, we had six children. When you got pregnant with Anna, I was surprised and thought we should be more realistic about raising a large family. Thus, when I decided to write, The Interpretation of Dreams, *we decided to use abstinence as a method of contraception. I understand that after six pregnancies, there was little likelihood that you would be able to relax and have much enthusiasm for your sexual partner, especially if he could not tolerate the use of contraceptives.*

Some of our difficulties came to the surface in 1896 when I was with my brother in Italy and you traveled to Hamburg to be with your mother. Maybe we needed a certain distance. Around that time, we received your sister, Minna, into our house. She was stricken by the loss of her fiance. Minna became an integral part of the family, which surely provoked some problems in the relationship between us and our children. I would say that her presence also brought enormous gains for the family group. I remember that you made some jealous comments about my relationship with Minna, but I know that everything resolved itself in the best way.

Sigmund and Martha Freud

I am aware that my participation in the education and supervision of our children was limited. I argued that the time at my disposal ought to be dedicated to work, leaving the care of domestic tasks to you. I sincerely confess my omission. Your performance with our children was protective and firm. Given a choice between reticence and clumsy interference, I chose the first option.

I know you were hurt when I said you had to tolerate the presence of the dogs—mine and Anna's. As I said, the dogs are loyal and sincere; when they like you, they are friendly; and when they don't like you, they bite. Human beings don't behave like this. By the way, I also think that your relationship with Anna was damaged from the time of her birth. Should we have had one more child?

I always lived a great contradiction. I wanted professional success, but the price would be maintaining an intense social life. Incompatible. In this case I considered you were by my side, either to provide support or because you didn't much like hosting all the guests. I always suspected that, though you fulfilled your domestic responsibilities to perfection, you did it out of duty and saw them as boring. They didn't satisfy the most vivacious girl in Hamburg.

My growing personal and professional ambition was always a way to compensate for these gaps. Martha, dear Martha,

I notice that the worsening of my pain distances you from me. I would like to understand your distance. In compensation, I sought even more closeness with Anna. In these final hours, I consider Anna's help indispensable. As you know, my will demonstrates my gratitude to our daughter and my colleague.

At the same time, Minna's participation in my theorization was very important. More than once, you referred to my theories as a type of pornography about which you refused to converse. One time, Anna told me that you, Martha, believed in me but not in psychoanalysis and that you said, "Women have always had this type of problem (neurotic); I don't see the need for psychoanalysis, though. After menopause, they become peaceful and resigned." Your modesty and timidity was reflected in your relationship with your mother; in that case, the difference from Minna's independent and assertive attitude springs to mind.

Our great friend, Ernst Simmel, once told me that if he had a wife with your qualities he would be able to write the same books as I. This comment contained a mixture of admiration and resentment. I regret that the majority of our children's names derive from my past friendships, which suggests that I chose them. Who knows if your choices would not have been better?

Your importance in my life became evident when, in 1919 during a pneumonia epidemic in Vienna, you contracted the infection. Your absence from the day-to-day activities of the family, left me extremely insecure. It goes without saying that I am talking about death. I know I am a hypochondriac. I always was. Years ago I confided in Fliess that not even you were aware of my delirium where death is concerned. On that occasion, I imagined various ways to die, and now I know it is completely different than I imagined.

Your mother's deaf opposition to our marriage did not

make me listen to her. With good reason, she wanted a better husband for her daughter, but, despite my not possessing a stable financial situation—or who knows if that was precisely the reason—she hoped that with the marriage you could rise, principally socially, considering that you belonged to the wealthiest Jewish community in Hamburg. More than once, I heard people say that despite living in Vienna for decades, you and Minna never lost your sophisticated German accent. Things suddenly became complicated with the death of your father, leaving to your mother the job of educating the children. You left Hamburg, but Hamburg never left your heart. Since Sophie's funeral, I never felt a great affinity for Hamburg; I never recovered from this loss and it saddened me when I remember that we were represented by Oliver and Ernst at that funeral.

Returning to Emmeline, I repeat that my relationship with your mother was never smooth, as you always knew. It began with her being an orthodox Jew, bothered by my atheism. When she became a widow, she sought to maintain control of the house with an iron hand, a fact that, in my opinion, augmented your divided feelings: your fiance or your own mother. Not even our letters could be sent to our respective addresses for fear that they would be intercepted.

At the beginning of our relationship, you impressed me with your interest in art and literature and your curiosity about the studies I was doing. That changed. By the way, that reminds me of the case of the painter, Fritz Wahle, who, despite being committed to your cousin, Elise, never missed a chance to court you. I always considered you a princess, but I never succeeded in being a prince.

During that period, I insisted on sending you a red rose and a poem in Latin every day, in this way assuring our imaginary royalty. I succeeded. After some delay, we married on September 13, 1886.

Freud, Martha, and Minna

In Vienna our first difficulties arose. The apartment in Bergasse was dark with very high walls and an old floor. And you managed to make if very comfortable, taking advantage of furniture that you brought from Hamburg and with the purchase of other carvings of dark wood, as well as the beautiful oriental rugs, crystals, and porcelains. The romance and poetry of life together were worn down, unfortunately, by the almost- -military administration of the house. I converted the tension into migraines that diminished after Paula arrived and began to help. Our conjugal life left the lyric phase and entered the epic phase. But, even so, I never heard your lips complain. Your approach toward the home evoked the Jewish proverb: "God could not do everything and be every place at the same time; so, he created the woman."

Martha, this letter aims to emphasize some significant points in our life. None of these events that I mentioned is unknown to you. At this time I want to show my gratitude to you for having filled such a fundamental role in my existence. I accomplished much, but only because you were back stage.

Finally, Martha, I want to ask you if, despite your religious convictions, you would arrange my cremation after I die and, following it, deposit my ashes in the Greek vase given me by Princess Marie Bonaparte on my seventieth birthday.

Good-bye,
Yours always, Sigmund

***

During the month of October, I received a letter from the editor of journal, *Time and Tide,* seeking my views on anti--Semitism, which has been on the rise even in England. Possibly due to my feelings of frustration at the realization that anti-Semitism could reach me here in my safe haven, I didn't respond until November, and then with a degree of irritation. I made a short commentary in which I related the dozens of years I dedicated to science. I spoke of the persecution that my family and I suffered and concluded, as justification for my departure from Vienna, a short verse from the French poem, "La Noue":

"The tumult suits the vain
The complaint falls hard on the fool
The honest man, when fooled
Departs without saying a word."

A few days after my response to the editor, Anna entered the office and told me that a reporter wanted to schedule an interview pertaining to psychoanalytic theory and its development. According to her, she appeared to be someone with a deep interest in psychoanalysis, who knew a little about the history and the theory and, beyond this, was in analysis. After hesitating, my vanity spoke up, and I accepted, arguing that the interview could enhance the British response to psychoanalysis. I received the journalist, and we spoke about politics and exchanged pleasantries.

She was young, appearing to be thirty-five, tall, and with unforgettable red cheeks. I decided to ask her if she would send me written questions, which I would address and respond in writing. I had several reasons to ask that the questions be sent to me. In the first place, I anticipated that the questions would be generic from a theoretical point of view and then might drift into aspects of my private life. In those days, I was in no condition to answer general questions, and maybe never would be again. With some effort, I would try to remember the difficulties. Frankly, I was depressed, weak, and discouraged, in addition to having great difficulty speaking and making myself understood. I feared, for this reason, that our conversation would become monothematic: The only theme would be death. But I still believed that my responses would be able to clarify and definitively bury some aspects of the past. The journalist's questions came in the mail, and I responded to them:

Dear Professor, it is my unequaled pleasure to interview a scientist of your stature. I know some points raised by the theory you created. I am also aware of your BBC interview in recent days and of your health problems. After all these years of extensive personal practice in psychoanalysis, from the time you worked with Dr. Joseph Breuer in Vienna until the current time, what is psychoanalytic theory, and what type of practice is it?"

Before anything else, I want to thank you for allowing me to respond in writing due to my precarious physical and psychological condition. As I have done at times in the past, I intend to take a pedagogical approach.

Your question about the nature of psychoanalytic

theory is very broad. I will respond in kind, with a broad reply.
I consider my theory to strike at
the heart of what if means to be
human. I believe that to explain
certain aspects of human existence, one must understand certain psychoanalytic assumptions.
As a physician, I was searching
for a way to treat neurological
and psychiatric disturbances. To
achieve some degree of understanding and scientific credibility,

Interview with BBC in 1938.

I found it necessary to rethink the way we organized the data
provided in the consultation room.

In other words, the models then in use by science had
proven too narrow and unable to account for all of the com-
plexity discovered by clinicians. Psychoanalytic theory requi-
red its proponents to abandon the rules, principles, and methods sacred to the existing science.

On the other hand, I often had the uncomfortable feeling that I was not achieving effects or discoveries that were
completely original. In truth, I was systematizing insights
about the human soul that had been described by earlier thinkers. Thus, psychoanalytic theory is simply a way to concep-
tualize phenomena long familiar to philosophers, artist, and
writers.

*How are theoretical concepts formed differently in
psychoanalysis than in other sciences?*

Put simply, psychoanalysis rests upon two pillars: (1)
the notion of psychic conflict and (2) its technique, namely
the clinical application. On the subject of psychic conflict, we

are talking about a theoretical framework, referred to as metapsychology, which is comparable to traditional metaphysics. To the students of psychoanalysis, the psyche appears as an arena of forces which are directed at diverse "goals," and the goals are often antagonistic. We don't have control over some things that exist at the point where the mind and the body overlap, i.e., at the boundary between the psyche and the somatic. Other forces are responsible for the existence of rules and norms that allow humans to live together in communities and societies in a more or less organized way; and finally, forces that, unfortunately, show us to our displeasure that we are not the kings of our own castles. What we call metapsychology, or psychodynamics, is the articulation of these demands or impulses, as well as a partial awareness we have of their existence. "Metapsychology," or "psychodynamics," describes the way these competing forces achieve an equilibrium. Unfortunately the result can cause psychic suffering in the form of neurosis, psychosis, or perversion.

With respect to the pillar of technique, I think it is based on language. Our access to these dynamic forces is made by the expression of emotions and affects through free association. The Unconscious contains forces which succeed in disguising and preventing rational understanding of affects, especially if we seek to apply our temporal and/or special concepts of reality, such as those proposed by Aristotelian logic. Logical-rational thinking loses any relevance in trying to understand the world according to its existential dimension, and this observation makes it difficult for conventional scientific environments to accept psychoanalytic theory. Logic is the enemy of psychology.

Another psychoanalytic notion which was equally strange to the *Zeitgeist* was transference. In our daily life, we frequently deal with a person or object, X, as if he were Z.

However, that confusion results in ambiguity, producing the lack of a clear and logical, cartesian definition of the person/object, which is always frightening to science." The analysts, I must emphasize, place a great deal of importance on language. Even I wrote at least one book dedicated to the examination of language and its "ambiguities." According to a current psychoanalytic concept, which is in its nascence, such linguistic phenomena are heard as metaphors.

I want to present these thoughts as mere suggestions for my theory's future direction. I am too old and sick for my current thoughts to lead psychoanalytic theory in new directions.

In other words, complete objectivity doesn't exist. When we speak, we have only the feeling and the permanent expectation that we will be heard and fully understood. Thus, in the view of psychoanalytic theory, contrary to other emerging linguistic theories, all communications are metaphorical. Needless to say, conventional science does not have sympathy for a phenomenological universe so disorganized and unpredictable.

Has some writer or philosopher already addressed himself to you discoveries?

No explicit reference occurs to me immediately; however, many anticipate me in their reflections. The philosopher Nietzsche wrote in one of his works: "It is not only reason, but also consciousness, that is submitted to our strongest instinct, the tyrant that lives within." It is difficult to disagree with this aphorism. Moreover, another reflection by the same philosopher is pertinent: "In true love, the soul embraces the body." Cicero also said: "Though it may sound absurd, nothing exists that was not said by someone." Finally, Pascal on the arrogance of the scientists of objectivity: "He who is without feeling is not miserable. A house in ruins is not miserable. When we put some effort to understanding misery, we end up understanding it."

Did you already try to identify the differences between your ideas and those of other thinkers?"

Considering what I set out to do, namely to create a theory, forty years was only a beginning, even with dozens of dedicated and faithful colleagues helping. When I began, I was impregnated with the scientific formulations of the era and with the teachings of Drs. Helmholtz and Brücke. I had a mechanistic view of nature and, more generally, of life. Even today I consider myself an inveterate rationalist. But, as I said, my clinical experience challenged me to look again at some of the pillars which sustained my practice. Though some people have in the past suggested that psychoanalysis was a type of home-made remedy, now we have evidence that psychoanalytic theory presents science with an innovative, alternative interpretation of the emotions and human suffering—one that definitely does not have its origin, not even its weightiest scientific support, in exhaustive descriptions of objective facts and measurable events. External events are secondary.

The raw material which concerns psychoanalysis is plastic, and its results reside in a continuous elaboration of subjective states. We have to admit that this way of doing science ends up being a source of mistakes and contradictions. In truth, to be human brings with it the germ of contradiction, and the interpretations we make in order to understand life remind me of the legend of the Hydra of Lerna. To transform the practice of analysis into an activity that seeks to eliminate human contradictions would be equivalent to destroying psychoanalysis at its origin—something like the English saying, "to throw the baby out with the bathwater."

What event would you consider fundamental to the creation of psychoanalysis?

At the moment I gave my patients a voice, I began to learn from them. One time a patient who was irritated with my verbosity said to me, "Let me talk!" This moment began the creation of psychoanalytic theory, which for forty years has wandered the desert of rejection. When I published *Moses*, I already doubted that the science which I was pursuing could facilitate the control of human emotions and actions. I confess that a new interpretation of my thoughts is recent, catalyzed by the writing of secular novels and by my illness, which reveals my finiteness.

With the advent of psychoanalytic practice, how will the frontiers between various areas of knowledge be established?

Psychoanalytic discoveries have received attention from very different fields of study. The theory that I created with entirely personal expectations now seeks, as I already said, to understand the functions of language, using study of people as both its point of departure and its destination. I feel a certain discomfort when I read a statement by Adolph Hitler with which, I have to admit, I agree: "Since time immemorial, the force that always unleashed the major religious and political avalanches in history was nothing but the magical force of words." I am exceedingly troubled when I recognize that the phenomenon of language can be used in many ways and serves many masters.

In the primordial years of psychoanalytic discovery, psychiatry embraced our thoughts as solutions to many of its problems. Even some colleagues and I shared in this enthusiasm. Now I see increasing division between psychoanalysis and the scientific ambitions of psychiatry, which increasingly attends more to biochemical issues than to the existential concerns of psychoanalysis. Sociology, on the other hand, without losing sight of its goal, succeeded in borrowing some group phenomena from psychoanalysis and employed them with success. Let's look to philosophy: In the past, it tried to divide the human experience into body and mind, or reason and emotion, or then into objective and subjective. Today it appears to recognize that this practice amounted to a logical exercise and resulted in a sterile syllogism. We see that now philosophy concerns itself with human problems *par excellance*, does not look for definitive and atemporal solutions. Philosophy, especially mixed with religious inquiries of an Aristotelian-Thomistic nature, is not comfortable with psychoanalytic theory.

Finally, I consider it extremely important to add that the connections between psychoanalysis and literature appear increasingly firm. In my recent statement on the importance of literature in the construction of the human experience, I insist on something taught me by novels and by my long life, which is nearing its end. As a matter of fact, I could observe *a posteriori* that most of my bibliographic citations come from literature and the arts; they are many points at which the two universes touch. Kipling said that the writer is trained to create the fable, but not the moral.

The writings of Franz Kafka, for example, are really lessons in psychoanalysis. His book, *Letter to my Father,* is entirely confessional, talks about bitterness, resentments, and sorrows felt by a son in relationship to his father. Beyond providing a catharsis to both Kafka and the reader who identifies with the character, it offers a beautiful opportunity to catch a glimpse of psychoanalytic phenomena. I already had the opportunity to argue that such insightfulness is impossible to teach. I mentioned Dostoyevsky and his unparalleled ability to create rich characters who reveal human contradictions and never made secret my admiration for Schnitzler, the doctor and former writer whose stories reveal truths about the human soul that psychoanalytic theory was never able to demonstrate. I consider it unnecessary to mention in detail the works of Cervantes, Goethe, Heine, and Rilke.

Professor, where do psychoanalysis, philosophy, and literature meet and diverge?

I could be making an assessment both intemperate and destitute of profound understanding, but I will risk saying that literature produced by classical authors almost always addressed themes of birth and death. I think that such occurrences are miraculous and remain incomprehensible to the human intellect. Religion attempts to address these issues, but I want to emphasize that I don't consider it possible to understand them with a vertical or transcendental approach, while Science approaches such phenomena by treating them through horizontal correlations. We know that to a great extent birth determines how a person lives; however, I have no doubt that the expectation of death also does this.

Recently I conversed with a Spanish colleague who participated in the introduction of psychoanalysis to Argentina, Dr. Angel Garma; and he introduced me to the work of an Argentine writer who was educated in Europe, one Jorge Luis Borges. Curiosity led me to read a story recommended by Dr. Garma. Fortunately, I could read Borges in the original Spanish. Many years ago, maybe around 1923, the year my illness appeared, I sent Sr. D. Luis López-Ballesteros, the Spanish publisher of my works, a little thank-you card and told him I could edit the translation in detail because as an adolescent I had learned Spanish when I decided to read Cervantes's great work, *Don Quixote*, in the original. Excuse this digression. I return to the Borges story. Titled "The Rigor of Science," it stimulated much thought. The little piece of fiction tells that "in a certain kingdom, art and cartography were achieving their apex. The scientific expertise resulted in the scientists creating maps which were increasingly detailed. Thus, the map of one province was made big enough to occupy the space of a city; and the map of the empire filled a whole province. This excessive scientific ambition made the scientists construct another map of the empire. One couldn't help but notice that this map was as big as the empire and occupied, inch by inch, the territory being mapped. The generations that followed were less attached to this type of scientific rigor and understood the uselessness of this exercise and abandoned the work to the ravages of the sun and rain. To this very day it is possible to visit the ruins that resulted from this ambitiousness."

Currently, what is your conception of science or scientific action?

I think the story by Borges addresses this question. Don't you? I believe he makes a fierce and ironic critique of conventional science, using literary fiction as a tool. It is true that some people treat literature and the arts with contempt or even as mere entertainment. But I think these are noble pursuits; they allow us unequaled opportunities to scrutinize the profundities of the human soul. Among the creative arts, psychoanalysis reveals itself to be a crude instrument which seeks to devise a method to reach the same end: to understand the deepest part of the soul. Unfortunately, I recognize this truth only at the end of my days.

How could one reach a better understanding of clinical psychoanalysis?

I beg your patience with this long discourse on the intimate relationship between psychoanalysis and literature and the arts. I offer it as a tribute and overdue recognition that psychoanalytic theory can borrow from the entire history of the arts. If in my youth I professed scientific rigor, these days I believe my understanding has broadened: I can't imagine what human drama has not been treated by the pen of a writer, the tip of a paintbrush, or is found in the carvings of a sculpture.

I remembered something else that did not come from an Anglo-Saxon source. Some time ago, I was reading the literary supplement of *The Times* when it called to my attention that the Portuguese writer, Fernando Pessoa, published prize--winning poems in English. I went to search for such poems and found, to my delight, others from which I recite some verses:

> *Science, science, science...*
> *Ah, how can everything be so null and void!*
> *The poverty of the intelligence*
> *Before the wealth of emotion!*
>
> *Science! How poor and empty!*
> *Rich is what the soul gives and possesses.*

It reminds me of another excerpt:

> *Just as the words fail when they want to express any thought.*
> *Just as the thoughts fail when they want to express any reality.*

Despite my debilitation, I suspect I have responded to your inquiry. As I have already said, literature fills the void between the intimacy of the unique experience and what is shared by all people. Just like the writer, the psychoanalyst gets all caught up in the filigrees of what is said or not said. The road to reach this stage is through listening—in the beginning, through the personal analysis, ones own inquiries, and then, cultivating a certain carelessness, or fluctuating attention—then formulating an understanding of one theoretically relevant fragment. In this way, the theory takes a trajectory which is unique to each patient and never before seen.

The continuous and obstinate exercise of abstraction as a resource aimed at obtaining knowledge creates a type of intellectual sedentarianism. As a result, we fail to pay attention to what is happening right in front of us and are content with merely pursuing an idea. This intellectual sedentarianism transforms the dialogues and discussions into circumlocution that ends up by leaving everything in the same place.

On the other hand, when I affirm a phenomenological intimacy between psychoanalysis and literature, naturally I cannot make the mistake of identifying the two fields as if they were only one. Thus, it is fundamental that we point out their differences or dissimilarities. As I said, the universes of literature and psychoanalysis have language as a point of departure: When a patient makes a free association or narrative, he does it with the aim of producing meanings that illuminate his singular identity, in other words, seek to translate his emotions and affects into words, unedited or anecdotal. In that case, the words possess a strong phenomenological quality, as I learned with Brentano. The compilation of his utterances takes the form of something resembling an intimate diary and is intensely influenced by the context. The narrative of the patient, we can say, makes salient his identification with the analyst and has as its objective the production of effects in the interlocutor or, if you like, in the listener.

In literature, and I speak of classical literature, words

aim to create a universal abstraction with respect to existence and the human experience. In the case of literature, a text principally seeks to transform a literary event into a recognizable social event relatively independent of context. When we make contact with a work of art, we identify with it; or with it as intermediary, we recognize ourselves in its characters and emotions. But such identification is merely intellectual, since it lacks the fundamental ingredient of an analysis, which we call transference.

Another important point pays respect to the place of metaphor in literature and in psychoanalysis. In literature the metaphor is understood as a figure of speech by means of which what is said gives up its literal meaning and takes the form of a parable or allegory. In psychoanalysis, the metaphor is the form that patient uses trying to interpret himself or the world beyond, including the analyst. The patient's narrative creates a story which, at first sight, does not

possess any relationship to his psychic defenses. In my opinion, the metaphor ends up being a type of trap in the battle between reason and affect. And sooner or later the affect wins. When the analyst offers an interpretation, the patient hears it and reflects secretively on what he has heard; at the same time he establishes a tacit agreement with the analyst: My sins were heard, understood, and are treated as if they belonged to someone else.

When I insist on the role played by language in clinical practice, I should share my fear that psychoanalysis might lose its way, returning to travel to roads previously taken when I adopted a scientific slant. In other words, I fear that psychoanalysis may come to abuse our discoveries concerning language, transforming psychoanalysis practice into mechanical and repetitive acts of positivistic sciences in an attempt to dominate the wilderness of creative phenomena provided by the

Word, transforming the method into stereotyped clichés.

After so many years, how would you evaluate the dissension that occurred in the original founding group of psychoanalysis? For example, especially in the role exercised Dr. Carl Gustav Jung?

Freud and Jung fishing on the coast of Reno, near Düsseldorf,
circa *1909*

Throughout an entire life dedicated to building the science of psychoanalysis, I was surrounded by friends who contributed much to the advance of the theory. Without a doubt, divergences and disputes occurred with various of them. Among all of my disciples, I consider Professor Jung to have been one of the most brilliant and creative. He immersed himself in studies and soon adopted points of view that diverged from the original concepts that I was proposing. I refer to some central points such as infantile sexuality, how the Unconscious was conceptualized, and the Oedipal complex. Everyone watched it happen; the tension between our positions was palpable. I was many times accused of not tolerating criticism or opposition to my views, and I admit that my difficulty intensified when this opposition became emotionally charged or personal, or one might say, neurotic. In the case of Professor Jung, the theoretical and conceptual differences were evident from the beginning. Today I clearly perceive that conceptual disagreements generated a climate unfavorable to the development of the theory and an irresolvable personal distance between us.

Existential human reality is kaleidoscopic, and it is completely plausible that someone armed with psychoanalytic concepts would propose to weave a different theory. In the beginning of the movement, I had great difficulty facing what I called the "deviations" of various disciples. Now, at the end of my life, I know that at the heart of psychoanalysis lies the reality that any event is multifaceted and subject to infinite interpretation. Fortunately or unfortunately, a model for existential human reality, nor for human conflicts, does not exist. Thus, once more I justify my affinity for writers, poets, and philosophers—creators of realities that will never come under the scrutiny of the conventional scientific method. Psychoanalysis does not offer a microscope, nor a telescope, much less a lens that could give a full view of life.

Nazism Finds its Scapegoat

A staff member at the German embassy in Paris violated protocol and burst breathlessly into the office of Ambassador Count Johannes Welczek, who sat, bent over, writing some notes. He lifted his head and with a disapproving look began to reprimand the employee for his failure to follow bureaucratic etiquette. Before the ambassador could finish his sermon, he saw the employee's agitated expression, realized something grave had happened, and let him speak.

"Excellency, forgive me, but I must inform you that our colleague and my immediate supervisor, Ernst von Rath, was shot five times at the Embassy door. The French police forbid us from taking measures because the attack occurred on French territory. The attacker is a young Jewish man, an illegal Polish immigrant, seventeen years of age. They are withholding any other information."

"Thank you. That will be all."

The ambassador subsequently made an internal call to confirm the details of the attack. His expression turned uncertain and hesitant. He walked to the window, opened the curtains, and watched the activity on the Rue de Lille. In front of the embassy, the traffic was unusual. He watched through the window for a few seconds and thought that the shots could have been meant for him. He continued observing the vicinity, letting his pensive gaze rest on the water of the Seine and the facade of the Louvre in the distance. He closed the curtains and picked up the telephone with a direct line to Germany. He sat down, listened as it rang, and someone answered.

"This is German Ambassador in France, Count Welczek."

"May I help you, Ambassador?"

"I would like to speak to Officer Heinrich Müller immediately."

The young German looked at Officer Müller and announced that the ambassador in France was on the line and handed him the receiver.

"Johannes? This is Müller speaking. What has happened?"

"Office Ernst von Rath just suffered an attack at the embassy door. He was shot five times. The attacker is a young, seventeen year-old, Polish Jew who was arrested by the French police. We cannot do anything, must less arrest the Jew. What are your instructions?"

"I am going to think about and consult with some people. I will return your call within a few minutes, but... Wait, is Rath dead?"

"I still don't know. Everything suggests that he did not survive. I am waiting to hear."

The ambassador hung up the phone and smiled enigmatically. He rose, looked into space, and thought, *Too bad this country-less Jew just provided a great service to the Reich!*

After about fifty minutes, the telephone rang and the ambassador answered without disguising his anxiety.

"Welczek."

"Müller. I am sending you a classified copy of the measures we are taking as a result of this serious, irreparable act. Our country is outraged by this unlawful and unjustifiable aggression perpetrated by a Jew who took advantage of French territory to harm a German official. I thank you in my name and in the name of our country for your attention and dedication to the cause! Follow the instructions. Thank you."

**

On the same day, November 7, 1938, the chief official of the Gestapo, Heinrich Müller, transmitted instructions to all Gestapo offices in German, a summary of which follows:

    1. Henceforth, these are entirely legal actions against the Jews, especially against their synagogues. These measures should be executed as soon as possible. They ought not, however, contradict the norms already established by the army; but, above all, the work should be accomplished conjointly.

    2. Any document considered important should be seized and confiscated from the synagogues.

    3. Arrest approximately twenty to thirty thousand Jews in the Reich. The most successful Jews should be selected. Regarding these cases, detailed instructions will be sent later tonight.

    4. During these maneuvers pay special attention

to those Jews you find to own or carry arms. The Gestapo will have responsibility for all measures taken. The synagogue of Cologne, as you know, holds material of great importance.

On November 10, 1938, new instructions were sent by the Gestapo, to supplement the plans already initiated by the Reich:

As a result of the assassination of Official von Rath in Paris, demonstrations against the Jews are expected to take place during the night. You must inform the political leadership and simultaneously execute the following instructions from the High Command of the Gestapo, adapting the methods to each case as warranted:

a) The suggested measures should be implemented only when they present no risk to German life or property. For example, the burning of synagogues should not threaten the surrounding areas.

b) Business, or any type of transactions with the Jews should be suspended. The police are instructed to supervise the course of negotiations and arrest any who violate these rules.

c) One should take special care in the streets so non-Jews are protected from possible harm.

d) Foreigners, even if Jewish, ought not be inconvenienced.

e) After completing the actions planned for the night, the remaining Jews—especially young, healthy, males—should be jailed and made comfortable. Subsequently, all will be taken to the nearest concentration camp. All jailed Jews must be well-treated in prison and during transport.

f) The contents of these orders must be rigorously obeyed since they originate from the High Command of the Reich.

These orders were followed rapidly and efficiently. The hunt for Jews had begun in all of the Reich, now officially justified by German authorities. According to assessments conducted afterwards, the operation resulted in the killing of ninety-one Jews, the imprisonment of twenty-six thousand, and the destruction of two hundred, sixty-five synagogues. Once more, history chose the Jewish people to serve as the scapegoat for its own difficulties. In this case, it was more ironic, since one of the most eminent victims was a Jew named Sigmund Freud, who among other contributions to an understanding of the human soul, described a psychological mechanism called projection, which consisted of dealing with unresolved psychological conflicts by attributing them to others.

Because these persecutions also involved breaking Jewish window panes and shop windows, this night came to be called Crystal Night. Adolf Hitler used the assassination of von Rath as justification to begin his persecution of the Jews. We were facing another holocaust, one that began in an absolutely barbaric way.

***

On November 29, the doorbell rang, and Annerl entered the office to announce another visit from writer, H. G. Wells. I immediately agreed he should come in. He sat right down and began to speak about the events in Germany and Austria at the beginning of the month. He also commented on an article on anti-Semitism, supposedly written by Arthur Koestler.

I noted that while commenting on the political motivations behind the persecution of the Jews, Wells emphasized the assassination of von Rath as the excuse offered by the

Reich for its actions—he lowered his voice and said that in Paris the nickname of the German official killed was "notre dame de Paris," due to his homosexuality. Thus, the political reasons for the attack obfuscated a crime of passion—the young Jew, Herschel Grynszpan had maintained a romance with the German diplomat and had been promised that his illegal stay in France would be make legal through von Rath's diplomatic and political intervention. He then said that there was a third version of the facts, namely, that young Herschel actually was targeting Ambassador Welczek, who previously had expelled his parents from Poland.

After Wells' comments, I told him that I increasingly believed a new pogrom was imminent. I had often been naïve, and politics usually bored me; however, in truth, the various versions of Rath's killing did interest me. Recent times were giving me a strange feeling that those adept at a science, or at least those with common sense, endlessly seek an ultimate, unique, and conclusive truth concerning everything that happens. They waste too much time using that perspective. Psychoanalytic conceptions of truth agree very well with various possible interpretations, even some that contradict others, without concerning itself over which would be the most true; in other words, the facts can be analyzed from multiple angles. In my opinion, in this particular case, it matters that the consequences of these interpretations do not diminish the tragedy of events.

I observed the writer's expression as it moved from pensive to worried. Naturally, I would never know what passed through his head. In any event, I finished: "During recent years, you have been dedicating yourself to writing science fiction, that is, books which are written by taking well-established scientific facts and extrapolating them, or using them as a starting point to create a new reality. You leave it to the reader to agree or disagree. I think that psychoanalysis works in the same way by extrapolating from, or elaborating upon, the facts. Who knows, maybe I write science fiction."

***

In the beginning of December, I received a visit from Princess Marie Bonaparte, who stayed in London for several days. She came to inform me she was having difficulty gaining the freedom of my sisters, who were still in Austria. I saw that the Princess felt discouraged and pessimistic about the success of her diplomatic efforts. If my sisters were freed, she could make sure they lived somewhere quiet in France.

***

The immediate result of the publication of my interview was, as foreseen, an insistent reiteration of the BBC invitation for another interview. Once more, I agreed; and it was transmitted on December 7, 1938. The recording lasted less time than the BBC hoped, and afterward I felt exhausted. Without doubt, my previous interview with the young journalist had been more coherent.

At this time, for some reason I talked with Anna about the analyst, Edoardo Weiss, of Trieste. Years ago, he visited us in Vienna; and during the meeting I told him that I had been mailed a copy of a novel written by Italo Svevo, *The Conscience of Zeno*. The novel was well-received by the critics in Paris, and Weiss had a close relationship with Svevo. The novel included an acidic critique of psychoanalysis leveled by the character, Zeno—an imaginary patient, who told of his efforts to quit smoking but couldn't. Soon after beginning to read, I could see that Dr. S practiced psychoanalysis in an erroneous way. The criticisms leveled by Zeno were had no basis and bordered on sarcasm. Now, it is no secret that I always had difficulty hearing criticism of the theory which I have conceived, especially when such critics became emotional. I reacted in a similar fashion when I heard the Australian satirist, Karl Kraus say, "Psychoanalysis creates a problem and then proposes to treat it," comparing psychoanalysis to some American missionaries when they arrived at the Lost Islands in the Pacific Ocean: After making contact with a native culture, they deduced that these "primitives" had not "learned" the concept of sin; then, the worried preachers doubled their task—first, blaming the natives for their supposed sins and, next, putting themselves to the job of evangelizing them. It was a comparison which sounded unjust and annoying.

Svevo affirmed that even if the intimate relationship between art and philosophy resembled a marriage of partners who didn't understand one another, even so they produced marvelous children. I inquired: Where does psychoanalysis enter in this negative critique on the relationship between art and philosophy? I always gave Weiss much attention and sympathy, and I was interested in his work in Trieste. I believed that his move to the United States was motivated by his difficulties getting established in his city of birth, possibly due to the fact that he was Jewish. Finally, I was tired of responding to criticisms, and I recalled the comment of Arnold Zweig when he said that the truth is unattainable, not to mention that humanity doesn't deserve it.

I felt increasingly ill, and I had trouble attending to my patients. I knew, however, that to interrupt my work meant, on the one hand, a type of surrender; while, on the other hand, it would leave me at the mercy of the disease that was consuming me. For that reason, in the middle of January, I accepted a young American professor for analysis. He would be living and studying in London for the next two years. He scheduled an interview and I decided to treat him, for at least two preliminary sessions.

***

I was seated, reading, when I heard two light knocks on the office door. I rose and looked at the young man, taller than me, carrying books and looking worried. I invited him in. He walked slowly to the center of the room, eyeing the furniture and waiting for instructions. He looked toward the couch and, as if he'd chosen his place, walked toward it. I told him that in the beginning he should sit in the chair in front of my desk. I asked him his name, and he responded, "Carl James." He sat down and looked at me as if he expected questions. After some seconds, I broke the silence with a coughing spell. Then, I fulfilled his expectation and asked, "Very well, Mr. James, what do want from an analysis?"

"Professor, I can't say for certain, but some colleagues in America said that since I'm an anthropologist, it would be important to engage in this type of psychological treatment."

"If I understand what you are saying, psychoanalysis would help you to function as an anthropologist. I agree. But I am referring to Mr. James; what benefit would Mr. James hope to gain from psychoanalysis?"

"Personally?"

"Certainly. I am speaking with James."

"It's true, despite thinking that my activities as a professor can be detached from my personal—-"

"Well, Mr. James, I can't so clearly separate human

activities. That separation depends a great deal on what you separate, doesn't it? So, what are your intentions?

"Yes, Professor, I agree, but before anything else, I should say that my belief in psychoanalytic techniques is not, one might say, firm."

"Fortunately, Mr. James, fortunately, in case we arrive at an agreement and you enter analysis, I assure you that the method, different from religious beliefs, acts independently of faith. In truth, although what I am going to say might irritate you, I consider your mistrust to be a sign of your difficulties."

"And what is the fee and duration of each appointment?"

"The fee is an essential part of the treatment, not only to remunerate me for an hour of work, but for a more important reason: If you pay me in accord with our arrangement, you can be certain that everything I do will be directed entirely by what you say to me and completely in your interest, although at the time, it can appear otherwise."

"Is this appointment preparatory or should I consider it part of the treatment?"

"Let's say we are arranging the pieces on a chess board, and at any moment we can interrupt the game."

"You mean to say that not only can I become dissatisfied with the treatment, but you can as well?"

"Exactly. As you know, it takes two players to play a game of chess."

"And how much time?"

"For the appointment or the entire process?"

"Both."

"Our appointment time can vary from a half-hour to a whole hour. As for the duration of the process, we can again compare it to a game of chess. I would say that we can know when we start to play, but it is not possible to foresee its course or end."

"Professor, excuse me if I hurry you. What is the essence of your method?"

"Make yourself comfortable. It has no essence, or, who knows, maybe its essence is so simple that is doesn't merit a name so pompous: We simply talk."

"Only that? That is very simple!"

"Mr. James, don't be so sure about the simplicity of our conversations. Many of our words serve to hide the meaning of others, even to the point of protecting our thoughts. Neither do they, the words, always serve a revelatory function."

"Should I tell things in chronological order?"

"Not necessarily. On the contrary, one more time I reiterate that your dedication to clarity can be seen as one more indication of your difficulties. Don't worry about a systemic or coherent narrative. I don't encourage that."

"What if I have a secret and don't intend to discuss it. Then what?"

"In that case, Mr. James, I would have to invite you to reflect on your secret in relation to me. In other words, what reasons would you have to omit something important to your life, especially faced with a professional that you chose to listen to you?"

"When you say that everything is treated as a conversation, can I ask or wait for your opinions?"

"Possibly... I might offer my opinions if I am certain that it doesn't serve my point of view. Do you understand?"

"I imagine that after some time, you will made a diagnosis."

"Certainly not. For the purposes of analysis, diagnoses are oversimplifications. People are much more complex. At most, after many meetings, I will be able to share some ideas with you, or rather, conjectures or formulations that, in truth, you will already well understand. Thus, a diagnosis will not be helpful."

"I come from an academic tradition. Thus, I tend to divide the human being into reason and emotion. In this room, will we treat our emotions using reason?"

"Excuse me, Mr. James, but you have just made a big mistake. I think it is fortunate that your doubt would surface at this point in our conversation. In this room, we give little attention to reason. The presupposition of the method is that reason, especially when it takes a logical or intellectual form, is bad counseling. I should say that to be human is to use reason with the objective of trying to hide what one feels. In truth, each word, even if spoken with a rational intent, never fails to be pregnant with emotion. Finally, I am saying that the human being makes use of reason, we would say, to defend against emotions less speakable or confessable. I am speaking with you rationally, sir. Who knows if it is permissible in this meeting? Soon we will abandon this practice."

"Will there be freedom to discuss any theme, say, scientific or professional?

"The meetings will be entirely guided by your emerging concerns. In truth, we should agree that your tomorrow is connected to your yesterday; and your yesterday, to your expectations about the future. It is a conversation without a predetermined end."

"Professor, the situation, I imagine, creates a very intimate climate."

"Without at doubt, my personality will change shape like a chameleon changes colors; and your affects could be compared to a machine gun shooting at random. From this climate we will seek to derive the advantage of a treatment; but, if you hope for a treatment in the medical model, you will be mistaken."

"But the relationship will be professional, won't it?"

"On my part, without a doubt. It is my responsibility to hear your emotional confessions or confusions."

"What guarantee do you offer that this won't become a type of 'friendship'?"

"None. If this occurs, it will be highly desirable to interrupt the treatment without delay, if possible."

"Comparing this to my academic training, you propose, as far as I can see, an asymmetrical relationship, much like that between a professor and a student. Is that what occurs in analysis?"

"According to my method and its presuppositions, it is not possible for anyone to teach something about our emotions, conflicts, contradiction, and affections. As you can see, this work presents a great paradox, but this may be its greatest strength."

"I am curious and afraid at the same time."

"It seems like a good beginning. I would like to continue the conversation tomorrow. What do you think?"

"I agree. At the same time?"

"You are scheduled for the same time. If something comes up to interfere, please let me know."

***

"Come in, James. Please be seated."

"Should I lie down on the couch?"

"Not yet. I want to talk a little more. Tell me more about what you do, your style of life."

"I have a normal life."

"I repeat, then: Tell me more about the reasons that bring you to analysis."

"In our last talk I explained some, but I do not know where to begin. I am married. I don't have children, and I left my wife in the United States."

"Very well, then tell me about your marriage, and the significance of leaving your wife in the United States."

"The reasons were academic. Two years pass very fast."

"Beyond this, to live in London, far from home and from your wife, can, also, bring a certain relief."

"It does, some."

"I can imagine that your coming to complete your studies in London also coincided with a marital crisis?"

"Yes, a small crisis. You appear to be guessing!"

"A risky supposition. A small crisis?"

"Well, a separation, that allows us to think about our situation and about other people."

"What other people?"

"My father-in-law particularly, and also my mother-in-law. They interfere excessively in our life, despite living in a different neighborhood."

"This interference bothers you, but how do you understand it? Or, if possible, give me an example."

"Well, despite our being married for three years, my wife, Beth, has never left her parents' home, not psychologically anyway."

"If she were in London, in your opinion, would she undergo analysis?"

"Only with difficulty. They agree among themselves that I am the cause of all of their problems."

"Them?"

"Yes, Beth, my father-in-law, and my mother-in-law. Ah, you asked for an example: They insist that we have a child. Their reasons are understandable, but I find my in-laws domineering."

"Your wife thinks as they do?"

"Yes, without a doubt."

"What prevents you from having a child?"

"I think we should have a longer period of time living together. A child always change a couple's routine."

"Yes, I cannot disagree. I understand that you would not like such a break in the routine. Or am I mistaken?"

"Beth is older then me, an only daughter, and spoiled."

"How do you get along with her parents day in and day out?"

"Fine. We are warm with each other. As times I suspect that there is some play-acting on both sides. In my opinion, Beth wants a child to please her parents."

"And what are your reasons to not want to please them?"

"Well, the child will be mine and not theirs. When I am working and spending more time at the university, teaching, she spends the day at their house; despite the short distance, that bothers me. We only see each other at night, and we hardly have time to talk. I am tired and when I lie down, I immediately fall asleep. She complains, saying that I don't give her enough attention. Recently we rarely have sexual relations."

"Is that bad?"

"What do you mean?"

"Is the sex bad?"

"I would not use that word, but our sex life has become a more or less mechanical ritual. She seems not to like it."

"And you?"

"I like it, and I don't like it, if you know what I mean."

"I don't."

"When we have sexual relations, I need to fantasize situations involving other people."

"Other women and other men."

"Yes."

"You are telling me very clearly."

"When we began to see each other, I didn't intend anything serious. She sort of obligated me."

"Obligated?"

"It is hard to explain. My family too. . ."

"Your family?"

"My parents, especially my father, would say that I should start a family soon, so he could take part in the children's growing up. My mother was always asking if Beth was pregnant, repeatedly, to the point of irritating me. She seemed to want us to have a child no matter what."

"You two?"

"Beth and I. Sometimes I thought that she was afraid that I, we, would not have a child."

"Afraid?"

"The fact that I would be a father meant something to her."

"To be a man, for example?"

"Yes, I think so. She wanted a family, and it seemed as if I didn't want to have my own family. I never felt close to my father."

"Suddenly you speak of your father."

"He was afraid to be close, physically. Do you understand?"

"Physical closeness is always difficult between men, ambiguous."

"To tell the truth, it frightens me, and I was always careful to prevent effusive displays of affection."

"You appear to be caught between two men on one side and between two women on the other."

"I don't understand."

"We'll come back to it another day."

"And, London suites me well. I feel free of responsibilities. I thought of writing letters every day, but I haven't. Beth has complained, and I tell her that my schedule is very full. I don't like to write. About my fantasies, yes, at times with men. You don't seem surprised. Is it normal?"

"Human."

"I should not."

"What we want and what happens are far apart. We can't control what we want."

I dedicated myself to James' analysis for some time with, it seemed to me, good results. In the end I was having great difficulty speaking due to the fact that my disease of the maxilla was advancing rapidly. Gradually James stopped putting all of his focus on anthropology and made his family relationships the priority.

**

In March I began receiving daily radiation therapy that resulted in uncomfortable collateral effects, such as hair loss and oral hemorrhaging. Also this month, when the Anschluss had been in power one year, Hitler invaded Czechoslovakia.

My constant companion, Max Schur boosted my confidence with his suggestions as a doctor and as my friend. I couldn't hide my disappointment when he told me he and his family had obtained their visas to the United States. Schur left on April 21 and told me that when his family got situated in New York and established legal residence, he would return to London. Some time later, the princess paid me a visit, and we enjoyed celebrating her birthday in our home. At the end of

Marie Bonaparte

June, we also quietly celebrated Martha's birthday.

I couldn't believe it when Max wrote that he would return to London so soon, and I was surprised when he arrived at the beginning of July, still with the same ability to tolerate my sulking. I decided, at last, that I would close my analytic practice at the end of the month and did so. I recalled something I'd said to Princess Marie Bonaparte: "Everything will vanish, even human thought." Regarding my thought, while voluminous, it would survive for at most twenty or thirty years. She argued that it was not true in the case of Homer, for example, whose thought has remained for more than three thousand years.

I responded, "Why would someone's thoughts last so long when everything in the universe will disappear?" I repeated the following irony, my old favorite, a statement that floats in my head and which I think captures the audacious and successful essence of American advertising: "Why live if you can be buried for ten dollars?"

***

20, Maresfield Gardens, London, N.W.3
8/6/1939

My dear Marie,

This letter will not make it to the mailbox. Your visit, which also will have been your last, left me especially emotional. Many times I referred to Martha as "princess." It was my way to show not respect, but my caring. I address myself to you as Marie to express caring and intimacy. This letter is written when I have all the time necessary to do it. It goes without saying that it will be my last, after thousands of letters written during my life. I closed my analytic practice last week. I couldn't continue. My body no longer obeyed my brain. The illness is superfluous now. I fully accept the necessity of death.

I have no news, and I write to show my gratitude one more time. I have no doubt that your presence in my life all these years left its indelible mark. I keep two photos of you between the books in my bookcase; it is very little, compared to your many loving gestures toward my family. When you gave me the beautiful urn from Corfu on my seventieth birthday, I showed my gratitude by saying that this present deserved to accompany me to my grave. Even knowing that this would make Martha unhappy, I asked that my ashes be deposited in that Greek urn.

As to psychoanalysis, would I say that you were the most special and dedicated ambassador of this new understanding. In England I had the luck to talk with Ernest Jones; in Germany, with Karl Abraham, and in France with others, like the unforgettable Mimi. As I always told you, today the world knows my theories, but my full recognition only took place among the analysts: Who knows whether my vanity stood in the way. See the vanity? Einstein had Newton behind him; but in the beginning I had no one behind me. I sought immortality, which evi-

dently means to be loved by unknown numbers of anonymous and unknown people. I understand that this ambition began not only through my work but when you believed that my confessional letters to Fliess ought to be preserved at any price. Don't be mistaken: After awhile I realized that the drafts I had thrown in the garbage were being carefully collected by Paula. She was following your instructions. I kept quiet. Those who don't have the privilege to share intimacies with the princess of Greece and Denmark refer to her as Y. R. H.—I wish monarchs could possess the elegance and grandeur of spirit that I found in you.

Many years ago, I received a letter from Laforgue, recommending you for analysis. I confess that I felt reluctant. Our friendship, now free of encumbrances, permits me to divulge that, in my response to Laforgue, I said that, considering my schedule, I didn't have time to waste on an analysis that did not have a serious objective. I was wrong. Soon I learned of your great interest, since childhood, in reports, stories, and happenings that involved assassinations and their motivations, the stories and novels by Edgar Allan Poe, for example.

Now, to look for the reasons of crimes and intimate sins that we commit is the purpose of analytic practice. Each time you visited me in exile—and you made many visits—I waited anxiously and full of expectation because you brought affection, dedication, and unforgettable presents.

Among my innumerable gaffes, one time, with reference to women, I said they differ from men in that they did not have the capacity to act as analysts: Their biological condition forces them to establish relationships that make them mother substitutes; thus, biology determines their destinies. Once again, I was wrong. You and many other women helped me to understand my point of view was mistaken. Today, I also think that to every analyst falls into the role of mother substitute. Even more, I find that the majority of my loyal and long-lasting friendships have been with women, even when I failed to understand what they wanted. Years later, I fought for your election as vice-president of the International Psychoanalytic Association. We won despite the fact you are not a physician. I consider this victory a small sign of my gratitude and my small tribute to the woman.

Spending time with you taught me many things, for example, that the opposite of naiveté is not intelligence, but bad faith. Your gestures revealed astuteness and the disposition to listen and speak without defenses, beyond your publicly stated conviction to seek the truth.

In 1925 we began your analysis, and I told you to be careful not to attach yourself excessively to me. I cited my advanced age and, ironically, exactly the opposite happened: I became consciously attached to you and I never regretted it.

Finally, Marie, these days I count on the presence and the lasting loyalty of Max, a great doctor, an unshakable friend that I had the good fortune to know by way of your indulgent hands. Once more, thank you.

Despite not believing in the omnipotence of thought, I wish you inner peace and many years of life.

Yours, Sigmund

***

Every hour of every day in August, I have thought about death. I remembered everything I read in this respect—reflections written by poets, novelists, and philosophers. Death was coming into view to show one more time that all men are equal before death. I read some place that Alexander Magno while riding with his soldiers through the dessert, came across a man in rags who was staring at a skull he held in the palm of his hands. His behavior intrigued Alexander who asked the poor man what he was looking for.

The man answered, "I try to find in this cranium some indication if it belonged to a king or a poor man. I can't find it."

On Sunday, September 3, 1939, at 11:00 a.m., Max and I were listening to the radio when a speaker interrupted the program to read the following communication: "From this date on, the citizens of the United Kingdom should be aware that His Majesty declared a state of war with Germany. Those young men who wish to volunteer should look for the enlistment locations on the posters along the streets. Young women and older persons can also participate in the war effort by volunteering at asylums, hospitals, public dining halls, and factories."

After the announcement, Max immediately warned that I should move to the consulting room on the ground floor. He advised that it would offer better protection from air attacks. I awaited the move while sitting in the bedroom, staring at my watch; I picked it up and wound it.

For the first days, it felt strange to awaken in the office. After awhile, perhaps as a consolation, I spent my idle hours looking at books and my collection of antiques. I read and re--read some of *The Manchester Guardian,* at the same time testing my capacity to tolerate pain. I heard the telephone ring many times and could not tell who answered, whether it was Anna, Paula, or Martha. They talked softly, gave news on my state, fearing that I would hear. I knew better than anyone else what was happening and could imagine what they were telling my friends over the phone.

REST IN PEACE – ז״ל

I am, as always, in the kitchen making tea. It is September 21, 1939. I hear unusual noises. I go to the living room and run into Dr. Max Schur, walking hurriedly, crying and with a bigger valise than the one he usually carries. Soon, Martha and Anna burst in, with tense, unhappy expressions. Dr. Schur looks at me and with a nod of the head excuses himself. Anna comes up and hugs me. I understand that the professor is dying. I automatically direct myself to the bedroom-office; and when I open the door, I see my dear professor in peace and breathing evenly. I feel relieved and turn to Anna who has followed me. With a look, I ask what has happened.

Anna informs me that Dr. Schur applied a strong dose of sedative to her father, with the objective of alleviating his pain. She also says that the professor had requested it, and she and her mother had agreed. The professor's sleep seems deep. I feel that we will never again hear his tremulous voice nor will we ever again see his penetrating eyes.

During the following day, and for all Saturday, the silence grew heavy. People were whispering to each other, maybe trying not to disturb the sleep and the peaceful rest of the man who fought bravely against his illness for sixteen years, enduring no less than thirty-one surgeries. Before and after each surgical intervention, we remained full of hope and faith.

On the morning of September 23, 1939, or more pre-cisely, at 3:00 a.m, the professor stopped breathing. His death  was witnessed by four wo-men who had been at his side for years: Dr. Jose-phine Stross, Mrs. Martha Freud, Miss Anna Freud, and me. I had never lost anyone with such meaning, who had always treated me with profound respect, often acting like a father, which made me admire him for his boundless capa-city to work and to pay at-tention to people of diverse origins. I could not imagine his death before it happened. Men like him should never die. During his years of suffering, I never heard any complaint, display of impatience, or irritation. He awaited the arrival of death as if waiting for a train to come in. And he left.

Josephine Stross

Anna told me that Dr. Schur gave the professor a strong dose of morphine at his request, and repeated it the fol-lowing day. Being so fragile, this action only made him sleep forever. She also told me that Dr. Schur left hurriedly that af-ternoon so he would not be present at the end, not to mention the fact that his family awaited him in the United States where they have emigrated.

The following two days were filled with many visits and homages. The letters have not stopped arriving, and I had to keep them in boxes to be read afterward and, naturally, to receive a response. I don't deny that after Sunday, the emo-tional atmosphere in the house was lighter and relieved. The

Anna and Freud

faces stopped looking so tense and anxious.

***

I am Paula Fichtl. I left my homeland, a village called Gnigl, close to Salzburg, in order to work in Vienna in
the home of Mrs. Dorothy Tiffany Burlingham as a nanny for
her children. At this time I was twenty-four. Mrs. Dorothy,
daughter of the millionaire Louis Tiffany of New York, entered analysis with the Professor and lived on the floor above
Bergasse 19. When Mrs. Dorothy's children became independent, I was let go and, and the same time, recommended to
the Freuds. That was how in 1929 at twenty-seven years of age,
I began to work with the Freud family. After some resistance
on the part of the women, Martha. Minna, and Anna, I began
to win their confidence, and everyone began to accept me as a

member of the family. I knew almost all of the Professor's patients, who treated me very politely; and, at times, they would give me gifts.

I knew ever corner of the house, the placement of ever object and, most importantly, the importance the Professor gave to each of his old art objects, which he held in the greatest esteem. The walls of the consulting office were covered with photos of different people, friends and colleagues. Strangely, there was not a single photograph of Frau Martha.

Paula Fichtl (on the left) and Anna Freud

When I went to live with the Freud family, the Professor was already sick, his daughter, Anna, examined him every morning. At the table, I noticed that the Professor always spoke slowly, due to the maxillary prosthesis that made him very uncomfortable and always appeared to be out of place. The presence of Anna in the Professor's daily life grew over the years. After awhile, I concluded that the Professor's marriage was peaceful but not necessarily happy. He was closer to Aunt

Minna, Mrs. Martha's sister, and he shared more conversation with her, much of which I did not understand.

I was often awakened by the shuffling footsteps of the Professor on his way to the bathroom to wash out his mouth and take care of his prosthesis. At that time he was still walking with some agility and frequently went to the antique shops of Vienna's District IX to look for some authentic, rare antique for his collection. When he arrived from these walks, he laughed easily and his eyes transmitted total peace and gentleness. Soon after my arrival at the Freud household, I noted that his work was internationally known. Important people visited almost weekly.

When I began to hear rumors of a possible move to England, I felt certain I would not be excluded from the adventure, which made me happy. While still in Vienna at the beginning of 1938, on the way to the bakery, I saw a swastika hanging over a neighborhood shop; and I understood the move would take place soon.

When we arrived at our final address in London, 20 Maresfield Gardens, I took care to arrange the furniture and decorations in the same places they had occupied in the house in Vienna. I wanted it to remind us of our homeland.

On the morning of September 26, the Freud family and innumerable friends and colleagues met in the Golders Green cemetery where the Professor's body was cremated in accordance with his request, though it violated Jewish tradition. The ceremony was extremely emotional. Two of the Professor's friends made speeches and praised him with words I will never forget. Dr. Ernest Jones, who socialized with the family for more than thirty years, began by reminding us of the friends and colleagues prevented by political problems from paying their final homage to the great man. He also said, "Those who witnessed the intolerable levels of suffering Freud endured in the final months should at this moment feel relief. We can say that Freud loved life like anyone else, and he never feared death. He died surrounded by affection in a country that received him with much greater courtesy, esteem, and honor than his own. And us? We will live in a world without Freud, a world without his vivid personality, without his fascinating and kindly smile; finally, without his always wise and poignant commentaries about the big and small things of life. I never met anyone who so loved the truth and hated the deceitful, the ambiguous, and the erroneous. He left life a great spirit. If we could say that someone defeated death, that he lives among us, this man is Freud."

These words moved everyone. Next, under a light, cold rain, came the speech of professor Stefan Zweig. I remember, also, some of what he said:

"Freud did not leave us, we are not at the end. It is only a smooth passage from mortality to immortality. Customs, education, philosophy, poetry, painting, and psychology—all the forms taken by the creative spirit and the dialogue between souls—for two or three generations, he enriched and changed them. Even those that never knew of his work, or who opposed it, are captives of the desire of his creative spirit. Here he is, in a time pretentious and forgotten, the bravest hunter of truths, for whom nothing in the world mattered more than the absolute, the eternally valid. He dared and dared, always alone, and one more time, dared to step where no one had stepped before; he gave us brave example of fighting the eternal war of humanity in the search for understanding. Freud achieved a profound harmony of two sounds—the firmness of spirit and goodness of the heart. At the end of his life, he achieved a most perfect harmony: a pure wisdom, clear, a wisdom of autumn. I am grateful for the worlds that he unveiled; and that now we cross alone and without leadership, always remembering you, faithfully and with veneration, you, most precious friend, the most loved of the masters, Sigmund Freud."

The ritual ended with cremation; and little by little, the people left in silence.

I imagined entering the house that held a particular memory of the Professor: the odor of his cigars. On the following day, I entered his office to clean each object and each book. He was no longer there.

***

The London newspapers reported his death on September 25. *The Guardian* dedicated almost an entire page to the creator of psychoanalytic theory. After mentioning his exile, it said that Freud's research turned dreams, things forgotten, and lapses into material for scientific investigation. It affirmed, too, that Freud would be recognized as a man who forced human beings, thinkers, and scientists to take dreams into consideration. Beyond this, his work flowed into many areas of learning and went beyond the field of medicine, producing a great quantity of research, extending from sociology to literature.

The newspaper, *The Times*, made a short reference: "Today we announce with sadness the death of Professor Sigmund Freud, M.D., creator of the science of psychoanalysis, who left Vienna after the invasion of Austria by Germany and the Nazi terror."

***

In the morning two days after the cremation, I was, as

always, in the kitchen when I heard Anna's slow, careful steps down the stairs and toward the front door. I went to meet her and saw she had a sad and serious expression. She carried a large leather bag. I asked her where she was going, and she answered, "To the crematorium." She opened the sack and showed me the black vase with beautifully drawn human figures. She said that the vase had been a present from Princess Marie Bonaparte, a Greco-Roman antique once used to store honey or wine.

Anna finished, "When he received the present, he told the Princess that it was so precious he should take it to the grave. I am going to the crematorium to watch while his ashes are put in this vase where they will stay; I would like my father's remains to be available for many generations to visit."

When I asked if she wanted my company, she told me she preferred to go alone and not speak with anyone. She left, head lowered, and slowly walked to the station to catch the metro that would take her to the cemetery. Suddenly, she returned and told me that she would take a taxi.

Later, she sought me out to tell that when she arrived at Golders Green, she found the person in charge of the crematorium. She told him she was Anna Freud, daughter of Professor Sigmund Freud, who had been cremated days before and she wanted some information. The man made himself available and told her that the ashes were ready. He took her to a room where a furnace performed the cremations. To the side was a closet with many bottles full of ashes. These bottles measured approximately thirty centimeters in height and were rounded. With a certain ceremony, he pointed to one of them, indicating it was Freud's. The man explained that after the cremation, the ashes were subjected to a process of homogenization and pulverized together with the major bones such as the hip. The temperature of the furnace reached approxima-

tely nine hundred de-
grees centigrade. At
the end, due to the
Professor's fragile sta-
te, his remains were
reduced to approxi-
mately three kilos. He
even said that future
visits would always be
supervised by an em-
ployee of the crema-
torium. This practice
was adopted after so-
meone stole the shoes
of Russian ballerina,
Anna Pavlova. Anna
completed her report,
telling me that she
carried the vase clut-
ched to her breast. She
asked that in the future he would move the ashes to a place
reserved for the family.

The ashes of the Professor stayed there, in the colum-
barium Ernest George. Many generations will visit the mortal
remains of my dear Professor. When I passed through the ves-
tibule of the house, I could collect the newspapers and dozens
of letters of condolence. The headlines of his favorite journals
noticed that, on September 27, 1939, the Nazis invaded War-
saw. The terror was only beginning.

Family Album

Sigmund at eight years of age, with his father, Jacob Freud, in 1864.

Freud with his sons Ernst e Martin in 1916.

*Freud and his mother,
Amalie*

Martha Freud, née *Bernays*

Freud with his grandchildren, children of Sophie

Freud and Jofi, one of his pet chow-chows, precursor of Lün, in his office in Vienna

This book was based on documents discussed by Freud's principal biographers. However, the story is fictional and is entirely the responsibility of the author.

Readers might feel tempted to distinguish the "true" events from those invented by the author. I anticipate such an endeavor will fail. The author suspects that the conception of facts in psychoanalytic theory is, itself, subject to different interpretations and creates confusion. Thus, it is appropriate to remember that in a letter to Fliess Freud, himself, said, "No reliable knowledge dwells in the Unconscious because it contains no sense of reality and cannot distinguish between a truth and a fiction that has been cathected by affect."

Written from November, 2005 to July, 2007,
in Belo Horizonte, Brazil.